The Good Conscience

BOOKS BY CARLOS FUENTES

Where the Air is Clear
The Good Conscience
Aura
The Death of Artemio Cruz
A Change of Skin
Terra Nostra
The Hydra Head
Burnt Water
Distant Relations
The Old Gringo
Myself with Others
Christopher Unborn
Constancia and Other Stories for Virgins

The Good Conscience

by Carlos Fuentes

Translated by Sam Hileman

The Noonday Press
Farrar, Straus and Giroux
New York

For
Luis Buñuel
great artist of our time
great destroyer of easy consciences
great creator of human hope

The Christian speaks with God,
the bourgeois speaks of God.
　　　　　　　　—Kierkegaard

On s'arrange mieux de sa mauvaise conscience
que de sa mauvaise reputation.
　　　　　　　　—Emmanuel Monnier

The Good Conscience

Chapter 1

They belonged, in the words of Uncle Jorge Balcárcel, to a Guanajuato family of more than slight accomplishments and decidedly worthy lineage. Guanajuato is to Mexico what Flanders is to Europe, the very core of a distinct style of life, and the preservation in all purity of tradition. An enumeration of the State's public figures would be endless, yet would fail to indicate the importance of political feeling in this region which boasts of being The Cradle of Mexican Independence. If one seeks the roots of the Republic's political system and patterns, one must go to Guanajuato. Here the delicate execution of devious plans originated. Here men know the uses of apparent and cloaking legality and are wise both in formal procedures and the tactics of smoke-filled hotel room maneuvering. Their ancestors during the centuries of New Spain were the students—and also the foot-soldiers—of Voltaire and Rousseau. Today their sons gather on the pompous stairways of the State University—in olden times a Jesuit center—to engage in discussions of Heidegger and Marx. Politically the men of Guanajuato possess a highly developed double faculty: an understanding of theory, and the ability to convert it into practical action.

The citizen of Guanajuato is, in other words, a practiced, talented, certified hypocrite. He is a lay hypocrite, as are all the best, and will serve whatever church seems in his opinion most likely to provide an efficient carrying-out of the theoretical "general will." Intelligent, coolly and clearly motivated while opaque externally, heirs to a tradition which Mexico's excessive political centralization has not destroyed, the men of Guanajuato represent the spirit of the Mexican heart. Seriousness that in Michoacan is streaked with solemnity, in Guanajuato is attenuated by irony and the sense of what is convenient. Zacatecas' provincialism is in Guanajuato leavened with universality: did not Baron von Humboldt visit here, does not the city of Guanajuato possess a Teátro Juárez which was decorated by the scenographer of the *Opéra Comique?* The tradition is that of the Century of Reason. What in a Pueblan is blatant hypocrisy, in a Guanajuatan is talented insinuation. What in a native of Mexico City is enthusiasm or reluctance, is pure compromise in the Guanajuatan.

The Ceballos family belonged to this singular heart of the Mexican spirit. For other families the key name in the history of the State might be Count de Casa Rul, or Intendent Riaño, or *Don* Miguel Hidalgo, or *Don* Juan Bautista Morales, or Father Montes de Oca. For the Ceballos there was no name more illustrious—witness the several portraits scattered through the rooms of their stone mansion—than that of Governor Muñoz Ledo, who had permitted the poor immigrant family to establish their clothing shop near the church of San Diego back in 1852.

The head of the house, *Don* Higinio Ceballos, had been a humble apprentice to one Baldomero Santa Cruz, a well-known dealer in woven stuffs on Sal Street, Madrid. He had learned his business thoroughly. A good cobbler sticks to his last—Higinio stuck to his counter and profited slowly but surely.

The Ceballos, Spaniards and moreover shopkeepers, were not looked upon with favor in that era of galloping Mexican independence. But the secretary of the governor of the State, when he encountered the obvious attractions of green-eyed seventeen year-old Mercedes, found reason to be pleased. She became Señora Lemus and arranged that her father's business should move from the shadows of the Alley of Dead Dogs to the sunny principal building across the street from the great church of San Diego. Naturally, the family always preferred to attribute their good fortune not to Secretary Lemus but to Governor Octaviano Muñoz Ledo, for in Guanajuato public relations have precedence over private truth.

Under such high auspices, the family could only prosper. The three sons received instruction from private tutors and learned those things which, next to practical business experience, are most important to worthy dealers in woven goods who are perilously rising socially. Not everything was rosy. Governor Ledo soon fell from power. But although Secretary Lemus had been a Conservative, he knew how to flip while toppling, and he landed securely planted in the field of Liberalism. In 1862, when Prim's Spanish army landed upon Mexican soil, the anti-Spanish uproar, led by youths who ran through the streets of the old city shouting "On to Madrid!," obliged Don Higinio to close his shop and hide with all his family—family of crinoline and curls, sideburns and cutaways, lapel carnations and waistcoat watch fobs—in the safety of the Lemus residence.

Even more than native Mexicans, the Ceballos clan were delighted when Prim departed. Business prospered again. At Ceballos and Sons, Guanajuatan ladies in pursuit of style could always find the latest and best in watered silk, Chinese shawls, or Brussels lace. When old Higinio died, the same day that Emperor Maximilian arrived in Mexico, his family was already well established in the provincial society.

The lordly residence in front of the church of San Roque had by this time been acquired. It was a colonial house, whitewashed, built of warm-colored quarried stone and walnut timbers. Thoroughbred horses clattered in and out of the wide *zaguan,* and in the stable were the black carriage for formal occasions, the Tilbury for outings, and the two seater for daily use. Grooms, maids, cooks and gardeners, music masters and tutors, hurried upon tight boots or bare feet through the long halls of the big dwelling.

The French invasion divided the three brothers. Pánfilo and José preferred to go on with the business, the former adhering without reservation to the Emperor, while the later professed in whispers the liberal ideas which had been the family's original motive for emigration to Mexico. Francisco, the youngest, joined the liberal struggle and marched with General Mariano Escobedo. He was captured in Jalisco and executed on the spot.

Don Higinio's widow, Margarita Machado, presided over not only the house but also the business. She was a wide-awake native of Córdoba, cheerful and unpreoccupied. Everything she did was done with an appearance of confusion, but the result was always perfect order and harmony. She was plump and jovial. The ladies of Guanajuato, unsophisticated and solemn, always had occasion to admire her. She kept up with the latest happenings in the great centers of fashion, received illustrated magazines from Paris and London, and was the first to display the bustle. She was intelligent, graciously intelligent: she guarded appearances and never let herself become either too sad or too happy about the varied events of daily life. This meant, carried to the extreme, that she was incapable of showing or asking for compassion. Shortly after *Don* Higinio's death she was once again to be seen scurrying about the marketplace followed by a servant, fingering heads of lettuce and cabbage, choosing pumpkin blooms and scented herbs, and showing off a brand new

Scotch plaid. Margarita considered herself an immigrant, no longer a Spaniard but not yet a Mexican. Through her example she tried to give her lesson of simple human honor to her sons José and Pánfilo.

"Who could have told me," she would say to them, "when Higinio began his apprenticeship in Madrid, that in Mexico we would come to be so prominent! Sometimes it frightens me. Don't forget: if we are anything in this world, we owe it all to honest labor. We are not aristocrats. We are merely a modest liberal family. Holy Virgin! Sometimes I wish the Santa Cruzes could see us now!"

Pánfilo always followed the words of his mother to the letter, taking her advice about what fabrics to buy, what patterns to feature, to whom credit should be granted and to whom denied. He was the hard worker, while his brother José—Pepe—was the shrewder. Pánfilo opened the store at seven in the morning and did not leave it except for the few minutes required to walk hastily home and breakfast with the family, and return. Pepe, on the other hand, liked parties, and would spend long social evenings discovering the clothing needs of the ladies and gentlemen present, so that on the following day he could have ready the cut or sample requested. He never arrived at the store until ten, and in the afternoons and evenings was always absent—teas, picnics on the lakes of Olla and San Renovato, card games. Occasionally he made trips to Mexico City. He lost the Madrid accent which Pánfilo, speaking with his teeth closed, clung to so tenaciously.

Pánfilo thought of nothing except the clothing store. But Pepe was waiting for a chance to look higher. Pánfilo died a bachelor. Pepe married, in 1873, Señorita Guillermina Montañez. It was the same year that Governor Florencio Antillon ordered the construction of the Teatro Juárez. The Governor's mustaches and goatee, his lustrous boots, his white trousers

and blue jacket with great lapels bordered in gold, shone
prominently at the Montañez-Ceballos wedding.

Pious, strict, without a trace of humor, Guillermina was
accepted rather than loved by widow Margarita. "Ave Maria,
this house is going to be as stiff as stays!" Occasionally, trying
to prick Guillermina a little, *Doña* Margarita would talk
about the dance-loving, witty and graceful girls of Andulusia,
but her words blew like Mediterranean spray across the
stone severity of her daughter-in-law. The Ceballos were
becoming truly Mexicans, and from the day Guillermina
entered the house it began to resemble a tintype. Out with
flowers and decolletage; in with high collars, stiff faces, and
solemn colors.

Guillermina Montañez was the daughter of an old family
whose wealth had been in mining. Mining had for all purposes
ceased during the wars of Independence, but loss of fortune
simply added to Guillermina's pride. People of the middle
class must, in order to feel themselves aristocrats, have something to sigh about. His wife's pretensions made Pepe more
than ever dissatisfied with his simple merchant status, and
he determined to rise. The revolt of Tuxtepec and Porfirio
Díaz' ascent to power decided his destiny. Montañez relatives
and Pepe's own friends came to hold positions in the federal
government, and Pepe multiplied his trips to the national
capital. These journeys made one thing very clear to him:
mining was going to come back. Díaz was offering assistance
in the form of cheap rail transportation. The latest techniques
and machines for the extraction and refinement of non-
precious metals were being imported. The demand for indus-
trial ores was increasing and would continue to increase.
Pepe convinced Guillermina—not without difficulty, for she
preferred looking back to leaping forward—that they ought
to sell their old gold mines in order to exploit new ones of
mercury, lead, and tin. Working in partnership with a British
firm, from 1890 on he received a very large annual income

from the new mines. Nor did that end his quick economic climb. The Land Law of 1894 made it possible for him to acquire, illegally, but with the acquiescence of the Porfirista authorities, 48,000 hectares in a region adjacent to the State of Michoacan, where he bought an additional 30,000 hectares, uniting subtropical crops with the wheat, alfalfa, and beans of Guanajuato.

In 1903 when President Porfirio Díaz passed beneath the bronze capitals and statues of the Muses to inaugurate the Teatro Juárez, the Ceballos family occupied one of the principal boxes. There Pepe presided, rosy, paunchy, resplendent with a graying beard cut in the style of the Emperor of Austria-Hungary. Surrounding him were stiff and haughty Guillermina and the always cordial octogenarian *Doña* Margarita; the hunched silence of the merchant Pánfilo, the obsequious attentiveness of the Lemus family who were now converted into poor relations, and the chatter of the two children, Rodolfo and Asunción, who were being allowed to stay up late for the first time. It could be said that this moment was Pepe's zenith. At the second intermission, Governor Obregón González made a little gesture that Pepe should pass to the presidential box to converse with Don Porfirio. During the last act many of the audience divided their attention between the mournful arias of the Ethiopian-Egyptian couple, and the discreet murmurs from the box of honor.

"Your presence truly honors us. This is a night that will not be forgotten," Pepe had said.

"Guanajuato is a bastion of Mexican progress," responded *Don* Porfirio.

"Tomorrow you will see beautiful fiestas. The Mayor has arranged everything most elegantly," went on Pepe, to whom the general remarks were incomprehensible.

"Good, good," commented *Don* Porfirio. "Let us have everything. Peace has cost us such labor that every Mexican has a right to divert himself now and then."

"Peace is wholly your accomplishment, Señor President," Pepe concluded.

After this triumph, there were no more great events in the life of the family. *Doña* Margarita died in 1905. Pánfilo moved from the big house of cut stone to rooms above the store. Poor hard-working merchant, without his mother he could not anticipate changes of style: bustles were replaced by hobble skirts, dark fabrics by fanciful ones, but Pánfilo did not notice. Before expiring the old lady had instructed him: "Keep your eye on what is worn by King Edward the Seventh," but Pánfilo did not understand, and his store was soon transformed into a solemn place to which customers came only in view of a funeral or some official occasion. With a certain ironical sadness he observed that his old clients now dealt at the shop which had been established on the opposite corner by another Spaniard recently arrived in Mexico, *Don* José Luis Régules.

The mansion at the foot of Jardín de Morelos was often the scene of large parties. Pepe Ceballos, true son of his mother, loved noise, the pop of wine corks, the whisper of violins and taffeta. Guillermina presented her exaggerated dignity as counterpoint, and for years these gatherings were the most talked about in Guanajuato. The city's gentility, families in government or in mining or business, others which had become affluent through cotton or flour or wool or leather, met again and again in the old colonial home. In the large salon on the second floor, where the old-fashioned decor had become French at the turn of the century, a quartet played the waltzes of Johann Strauss, Juventino Rosas, and Ricardo Castro, servants hurried with trays, and there were even political discussions. Two groups generally formed: one consisted of government functionaries and businessmen and mine-owners, and was the larger; these gentlemen applauded every aspect of the Díaz regime. In the other group were the new industrialists who asked for certain changes, greater freedom, new minds around the president. But all of them respected Díaz profoundly and considered him indispensable.

From time to time there would also be parties for the children. Rodolfo, the elder, in time would become a lawyer. Pepe had already confidently enrolled him in the Catholic Law School for the year 1912. Doña Guillermina expected to marry off Asunción, the daughter, at the age of eighteen, and with this in mind cultivated the little Balcárcel del Moral boy, who was the heir of another rich family.

One night in 1910, Guillermina received word that her husband—so ruddy, so healthy—had fallen with a terrible fever in a village near León. He had been three days traveling his estate on horseback. Night and a violent rain storm had descended upon him together. He was dying of pneumonia, and so delirious that it was impossible to move him from the dirty adobe hut where he lay. Proud Guillermina hurried to him, only to find, upon arrival, the peon's dead fires, the mourning neighing of horses, and Pepe's body. It would appear that the Ceballos patriarchs were accustomed to dying on historic dates, for this was a morning in the third week of November and soon afterward it was known throughout the region that on the same day Madero had risen in revolt in San Luis Potosí.

The funeral procession, headed by the widow and the two black-clad children, had just dissolved when Pánfilo drew near his sister-in-law and informed her that she could count upon him as the man of the family. Guillermina paused at the exit to the Municipal Cemetery, facing the compact panorama —brown, green, and black—of mountains, glens, and churches. She reflected that she would not go far relying upon the judgment of the aged clothier. She would have to trust her own good sense to resolve the problems caused by her husband's death. She was sad and a little troubled, but at the same time felt lighter, for sadness was the feeling she most enjoyed. Taking Rodolfo and Asunción by the hand, she boarded the black carriage and rode home.

Shortly thereafter, she sold the mines to Pepe's British associates at a very good price indeed, and entrusted the vast hacienda to an administrator. She decided to wed Asunción three years earlier than planned before, at fifteen, and to prepare Rodolfo to take his father's place. She was glad to rid herself of the mines, in whose exploitation, sweaty, tyrannous, often criminal, the first wealth of her ancestors had been founded . . . lords of the manor but not of the manner, men of rough words and quick whips. She was going to limit herself to landowning; it was like stepping from a muddy street to the sidewalk. Rodolfo's projected law career was abandoned. It would be enough for him to handle the hacienda. But if the unlinked events of the already busy revolution were incomprehensible to her, even more so was her son's character. It seemed that the Andalusan *Doña* Margarita had been resusitated to infuse, in a disagreeable and accentuated way, the boy's physical appearance and spirit. No one was less worried about anything than Rodolfo Ceballos. No one was less suited for the management and discipline of large landholdings.

In the beginning the Revolution did not frighten *Doña* Guillermina. It spread down from the north, and in 1914 Guanajuato began to fill with refugee families, many of them old friends, from Coahuila, San Luis, and Chihuahua. Relatives, former business associates of *Don* Pepe, and friends of friends poured in. Social life quickened, and Guillermina found this pleasant. There were balls and parties, and everyone attended the usual religious festivities. From time to time someone spoke of violence and killing: Guillermina would reply placidly that this was not the first revolution they had known: "Guanajuato has always been the richest state in the

Republic, the granary and the treasury of Mexico, as my husband used to say, and no one will dare to disturb us here."

Events turned out otherwise. A band of revolutionists took over, the next year, Don Pepe's land. They emptied the corn bins and barns, and Rodolfo, who was living at the hacienda by now, informed his mother that the situation was grave. For the first time Guillermina felt afraid. The worst was still to come. In 1916 Villa approached Guanajuato with nine thousand men. Young Asunción, only fifteen years of age but already married, fled with her husband, and the stone mansion was empty except for Guillermina and Pánfilo. The elderly merchant closed his store to keep from accepting the paper money printed by the different factions. Then Obregón arrived and forced the store to be opened again. He also required salaries to be raised. Uncle Pánfilo believed he was going to go bankrupt. *Doña* Guillermina hid her gold pesos under the floor of her bedroom. Suddenly all of this seemed unimportant. The gentility died of fear when Obregón abandoned the city. Guillermina and Pánfilo shut themselves in and piled mattresses against the windows. General Natera was about to appear with Villa's troops. Then both sides went away to join in battle at Celaya, and the city was left in the hands of the bandit Palomó. There was continuous sacking, gunfire at all hours. For the Ceballos, it was like the end of the world.

Doña Guillermina did not completely lose her head. She relieved Rodolfo of his duties at the hacienda and took its administration into her own hands, arranging for thirty armed men to guard the burned buildings. Her religious activity multiplied. She did not miss a single procession in favor of peace. She lit candles in every church in favor of peace; she wept in her bedroom in favor of peace, she recited Salve Reginas in favor of peace. At the same time, her hunger to look back lovingly on the past was fed by the terrible events of the present. Although she wailed, in public, because the ringing of church bells during the fiestas of the Holy Virgin had been prohibited, privately she doted sweetly upon the memory of how those bells had echoed in better times. Openly she wept the expulsion of the Sisters of the Good Shepherd; alone she recalled with pleasure the generosity which the Ceballos had always heaped upon the nuns. She was scandalized that deceitful Siurob had dared to take the portraits of President Díaz and Governor Obregón Gonzales down from the walls of the governor's palace; but what delight she felt remembering *Don* Porfirio with Pepe at the opera, and *Don* Joaquín witnessing Asunción's wedding!

Under the governorship of Siurob, the unrest settled. Almost without being aware of it, Rodolfo Ceballos found himself going to the store every day. Uncle Pánfilo rarely visited it now. The wrinkled, lisping old man, who was about to reach his eightieth birthday, let Rodolfo handle everything, and Rodolfo found his true road in life, his heriditary role, which was to preside, with bonhommie, behind a counter.

Few servants were left in the mansion in 1917, when Pánfilo died. Almost all the bedrooms were closed in 1920, when Guillermina followed him. Asunción and her husband, Jorge Balcárcel, were living in England. Rodolfo, all alone, closed more doors. The new Agrarian Reform Law resulted in the loss of a good part of the 78,000 hectares which Pepe Ceballos had acquired so cheaply. Rodolfo was indisposed to struggle; he crossed his arms and let the land go. With the store and with the gold pesos his mother had left, the last Ceballos could live very comfortably. His tendency to obesity, inherited from his grandmother, was accentuated by his sedentary life, and at twenty-nine he was a rotund young man, drowsy and pleasant, who made friends with everyone except the descendents of the old families who had used to gather in the stone mansion. These ruined aristocrats filled him with disgust. All they could do was talk about the good old days. They had all suffered bitterly from the Revolution, they all lamented it; many of them departed to live in Mexico City. Rodolfo much preferred to discuss the price of cotton or the magnificent sardines which *Don* Chepepón López sold, or memorable games of dominoes played with other merchants in the bar of the Jardín del Unión park. It was to the Jardín that he went when he closed the store at six each afternoon. In a short time, unrestrained by family, the only inhabitant of the mansion, he began to invite his rather surprised Jardín companions home. It would be hard to imagine what *Doña* Guillermina would have said if she could have seen those gatherings of men in their shirt-sleeves beneath her French chandeliers. They smoked cigars. They drank beer. They talked about market prices and played dominoes.

But it was thanks to these friends, in particular to the aforementioned *Don* Chepepón López, provendor of wines and canned goods, that Rodolfo met the woman who was to become his wife and the mother of his son. Adelina López was a tall, shy, simple young girl, much given to attending novenas, to receiving communion on First Fridays, and to shutting herself up in seclusion during Lent. Rodolfo had seen her various times at the serenade which was presented three times a week in the Jardín del Unión. The young men would promenade in one direction around the park, the young women in the other. Rodolfo merely sat on a bench with a toothpick between his lips, and observed. In reality the girl neither pleased nor displeased him. What with his work, his friends, and an occasional visit to a bordel, he lived quite contented. If it had not been for *Don* Chepepón's ambition to see his daughter installed as mistress of the mansion at the foot of Jardín Morelos, Jaime Ceballos would never have been born.

Señorita López began to appear frequently in Rodolfo's store. He loved to talk, so he enjoyed her ponderous conversations about the sanctity of the home, and the importance, in a mother, of good Christian training. Soon the plump

merchant found himself invited on shabby picnics and excursions, to the lakes behind Guanajuato's dams, to the old
mining center, now a ghost town. Adelina murmured an
alarmed repulse, but soon allowed the nervous and drowsy
young man to hold her hand. When at last their friends
observed them entering the church of the Compañia together one First Friday, all were sure that *Don* Chepepón
had gained his victory.

Not without setbacks, however. The future groom wrote
to his sister in England. Asunción replied stating that she
did not know who the López family were but that Balcárcel,
her husband, believed that Chepepón was of very dubious
ancestry. When that failed to dissuade Rodolfo, she wrote
again announcing that the daughter of a *Don* Nobody was
not going to sleep in her mother's bed. The truth was that
Chepepón López had in his youth been a humble apprentice
in the shop of that very *Don* José Luis Regules who had given
Uncle Pánfilo such ruinous competition. Young Chepepón
had sired a natural daughter, who he legitimized, and this
was Adelina.

"But Grandfather Higinio began as an apprentice too,"
Rodolfo told himself.

In December of 1926 the marriage took place in the stone
mansion, to the merry-making of Rodolfo's Jardín companions. Almost immediately after the wedding, Rodolfo decided that he ought to maintain, insofar as was possible, the
familiar appearance of a Ceballos. Marriage imposed a moral
change upon him, and the only change possible was to give
up the friendly, lazy, unworried life he had until this time enjoyed, and to become—how did he say it himself?—more
thoughtful, more serious. No one had ever had faith in him.
He had not been permitted to study law. His mother had
taken the hacienda away from him just as he was learning
to manage it. Now he would prove that he could be just as
good a head of a family as his father. The transformation was

not very difficult, for if he was the grandson of Margarita the jolly, he was also the son of Guillermina the stiff.

And in truth, Adelina did what she could to push him in this direction, an action which on her part was suicidal. The moment Rodolfo assumed a stricter social standard, he was inevitably going to be displeased and eventually disgusted by her vulgarity. Her chance for happiness, though she did not understand it, lay precisely in keeping him lazy and easy-going: she was the ideal wife for a beer-drinking dominoes player. Nevertheless, it was she who persuaded him to close the house to his old friends. It was she who ruled that *Don* Chepepón could visit only on Sundays. It was she who insisted they must open the enormous French drawing room again, and it was she who prepared the select guest list for their frequent entertainments. She suggested that Rodolfo hire a clerk to stand behind the counter in the store, so that he might retire to a lonely upstairs office. It was Adelina, in short, who took the eternal smile from her husband's lips.

The parties which Adelina and Rodolfo gave were too strained to be successful, and for Adelina personally they were catastrophes. Her husband was forced now to make comparisons. It was not that the breeding of their guests was so exemplary, but that Adelina's was so deficient. She fell far below even the standard of provincial mediocrity. All voices were coarse; hers was shrill. All of them were hypocrites; she was a super-hypocrite. All pretended piety; Adelina did so with bad taste. All of them possessed at least the minimal knowledge of established forms which was wholly lacking in her. Talk about her abounded: she was common, shallow, tactless, above all, ill-bred. And Rodolfo, holding now to the family's old traditions, had to agree. Adelina made her social splash, such as it was, but lost her husband's affection. Quarrels began, and weeping.

Chapter 2

In 1927 THE BALCARCELS RETURNED from England. Rodolfo, caught between the rock of his new independence and the unhappy sea of his alienation from Adelina, suggested that they make their home in the big house for a few weeks at least, and when Asunción saw what the situation was, she agreed. Immediately she began to discover alarming defects in Adelina. The floors were dusty, the silver was not polished, there were cockroaches in the pantry.

Jorge Balcárcel del Moral, the young man who at twenty had fled Guanajuato in terror upon hearing the hooves of the revolutionary cavalry, had studied for years at the London School of Economics, and was back in Mexico now with a cloud of degrees and scholarly honors. President Calles was just beginning to reorganize the finances of the nation; he found Balcárcel prepared to help, and entrusted him with a detailed economic study of the State of Guanajuato. One day, wearing his narrow trousers and his Scotch-plaid cap, the inexperienced economist asked the plump merchant to give up his home.

"Decidedly, the nature of your obligations allows you to live in very comfortable rooms above the store, as Uncle

18

Pánfilo did, while the nature of ours requires the family residence. My duties force me to make the highest possible social presentation. While yours . . ." And from that moment Barcárcel's voice was stiff with authority.

Adelina dared to oppose him at first. "No, *señor*. What you don't realize is that Fito and I also have social obligations with the best people in Guanajuato. We receive them here, just as in the time of Guillermina. *Sí, señor*."

But Rodolfo, significantly, said nothing, and two months later, overwhelmed by Asunción's peculiar helpfulness— "Come, my dear, it will be better if I arrange the dinner party this time. Everyone laughs at you, you know. It's just that there are certain things you didn't learn when you were small."—and by her own sense of inferiority and helplessness, Adelina announced that she was going to visit her father for a while. Rodolfo did not detain her. When the next month *Don* Chepepón came to the store and informed him that Adelina was expecting a child, Rodolfo felt repentant and wanted to see her. But his sister immediately made it plain that the course of wisdom would be to take the child but let the mother go, to annul a marriage so contrary to good sense, so that some day he might take a second wife worthy of his name and situation.

Rodolfo passed several miserable nights trying to decide what to do. One moment he felt himself the unworried and good-natured young man of old; the next, he was the serious minded gentleman. One moment his heart was full of tenderness for his wife; the next, he was sure that Asunción was right. He grew sad thinking of Adelina giving birth alone. Then he remembered her horrible mismanagement of the house, her vulgarity, her love of mere appearances. And as he struggled first one way and then the other, it was Asunción who was always present to help him to do nothing at all, and it was Asunción who finally introduced him to the blond little baby who was as rosy as Grandfather Pepe. She said nothing about the mother, and Rodolfo did not dare to ask. Only he and the Balcárcels attended the baptism. The infant soon learned to cry "mama" to Asunción.

Rodolfo had given up the master bedroom when Adelina left and had moved to the bedroom adjacent. Now Asunción wanted the baby there. She pointed out to her brother that his bachelor habits made it convenient for him to live in a more isolated part of the house. The servants' quarters were on the patio floor. An spiral iron stairs, open to the weather, corkscrewed up one wall to the high *azotea* where, on the roof, Rodolfo now had his room. Only the clatter of the flimsy stairs announced every night his slow climb. He puffed and panted. Sometimes his head whirled and he was afraid he would fall. But his effort had recompenses: how lovely Guanajuato was at night, what forgotten lights flickered from the soft colored villages, from the mountains, from country fires. And the isolation of his room made it easy for him to escape *Doña* Asunción's guests. Rodolfo soon grew accustomed to his position far from the domestic center of gravity. He returned to the bar of the Jardín del Unión, to his Saturday night visits to the bordel, to his Sunday beer.

Uncle Balcárcel, in order to prepare his famous economic study, established relations with the city and state politicians, whom he shocked by his expositions of English economic doctrines. If armed revolt had filled him with terror in 1915, in 1929 the Official Revolution found him an energetic supporter. "Build" was the Revolutionary slogan now, and President Calles was carrying it out. There was a great contrast between Balcárcel's rabidly anti-clerical attitude in public, and his domestic piety. Asunción's virtues, in this latter respect, exceeded those of all her ancestors. She was the first in the city to arrange a private chapel in her home during the years of religious persecution. It was interesting to observe Balcárcel orating in the Jardín del Unión against the conspiracy of the priesthood, and to see Asunción, the following day, carrying images of the Virgin into the great stone mansion. The truth was that *Señor* Balcárcel always took part in the evening religious devotions which his wife, following the example of her mother, held for the household. Heiress to so many Christian virtues, Asunción recalled with horror the way her grandmother, the Andalusan Margarita, had scoffed about these ceremonies and had declared that God is honored in one's heart, not by external show. She had been in her dotage, poor old woman! The contradiction between her husband's public and private attitudes about religion, on the other hand, disturbed Asunción not at all. That was, she understood, a male matter in which a wife ought not to interfere. Moreover she knew that good political connections had always been the family's economic salvation, and she was not so foolish as to suggest that a concrete and present good be sacrificed for a moral and theoretical one, especially when both could so easily be retained. Did not the Ceballos owe their fortune and their position to the friendship of Governors Muñoz Ledo and Antillón? Had not their wealth been augmented and their social status assured thanks to the good will of President Díaz? Why should they now alienate themselves from President Calles? Or from President Avila Camacho, during whose administration Jorge Balcárcel finally permitted himself the luxury of synchronizing his private faith with his public declarations. "I always said," he would then explain, "that like wine, the Revolution would improve with age. Decidedly we have passed the period of excesses." In this way, and thanks to this philosophy, he was able to be, successively, a local legislator, a director of a bank, and from 1942 on, a prosperous money-lender. In the old days the big house had possessed twenty bedrooms. Balcárcel chained the doors that led to the right wing, opened a narrow entrance from the alley of San Roque, and rented rooms. Thus began his career as a landlord, which, along

with his political activity and his money-lending, was to be
the principal source of his provincial fortune.

For Balcárcel's family had consumed their wealth—relative
wealth, measured by the time, 1910, and the place, a Mexican
province—in supporting with decorum the English migration
and studies of the only son. Many tons of ore had been converted into steamship tickets, London apartments, suits and
dresses, economics textbooks, for Jorge Balcárcel and his
young wife Asunción Ceballos. Forced land sales did not
allow the best price. When Jorge returned to Guanajuato,
his impoverished state obliged him to forget past glory and
struggle to re-attain the wealth and power expected of a
Balcárcel. Upon completing the study for Calles, he gave up
all serious interest in the science of economics. There was no
one with whom to discuss those esoteric topics—cartels, co-
efficients of income, public debt. He forgot his English degrees and dedicated himself to the assiduous cultivation of
the new revolutionary regency. He opened the doors of the
Ceballos mansion to people who a decade earlier could not
have dreamed of entering there. He was a deputy in the
State Legislature and although his performance was unre-
markable—or perhaps precisely for this reason—he was
offered the opportunity to go to the Federal Chamber of
Deputies.

He declined: "Decidedly, I cannot abandon my little native
state and its many problems," he declared officially. Inwardly
he was thinking about the uneasy parades of ghosts from the
time of Díaz he would meet in the national capital; that the
presence in the Federal Legislature of an ex-mine owner and
landlord might create trouble. He suspected that in a great
city he would encounter the danger of living unknown as
merely another ruined aristocrat. In Guanajuato, on the other
hand, he could become powerful. He contented himself with
juicy commissions on contracts for public works, and a little
later with the directorship of the bank. Advised in advance

of the successive currency devaluations, intermediary in many of the state's contracts and fiscal operations, a careful money-lender, in fifteen years Balcárcel accumulated a tidy fortune. From his ancestors he inherited the habit of safeguarding a large part of his wealth in foreign banks; from the Revolutionary oligarchy he learned to invest in urban real estate. Between interest and rental income, he had very easily enough to live in the highest luxury.

See him thus: height average, hair curly and thinning, lips thin and compressed, complexion bilious, cheeks hanging from jutting cheekbones; small sharp eyes, an air of solemn intellectuality, always scrupulously clean-shaven. He is sententious, given to invoking moral maxims at every moment, and to hooking his hand in his vest in an imperial gesture. Suits very conservative, almost old fashioned; false teeth, bifocals. If for a long time he has had to sacrifice his religious piety to political expediency, now that he can publically declare himself a believer he does so over and over, and the words "Catholic" and "the upper classes" are synonyms to him. Religious rhetoric he uses to justify his worldly interests: "Decidedly, private property is a postulate of Divine Reason." "In Mexico, we of the upper class have the obligation to take charge of the morals, the education, and the economic activity of a people who are decidedly backward." "A man's treasures are his family and his faith." Such are his more frequent and felicitous sayings. He is a man of exact hours, and will not tolerate unpunctuality or the slightest change in established habits any more than he will condone frivolity of speech. At seven-thirty in the morning he must have his hot bath and at eight an egg boiled for exactly one hundred and eighty seconds. His laundry for the week must be laid out on the bed so that he may count it personally and inspect the amount of starch in the collars. In his presence, conversation must always be steered toward those familiar topics upon which he can make a pronouncement. In his home, Rosary

must be exactly at six in the evening, and on Sundays everyone must wear black. But above all, he may not be contradicted and he must always be respected. And he is respected.
His raised index finger is a symbol of confident authority.
Every night he can go to bed with his magazines—his only
reading—and an infinite sense of righteousness, tranquility,
and power.

Like all bourgeois Catholics, Balcárcel was really a Protes-
tant. If in the first instance the wide world was divided into
good beings who thought as he did and sinners who thought
otherwise, in the second, the local world of Guanajuato was
divided into decent folk who possessed wealth and evil beggars who did not. Carrying this Manichaean attitude into the
bosom of his family, Balcárcel became the strict head of the
house who understood righteousness, while all others in
the mansion were more or less suspects whom it was necessary to watch closely and prod toward good behavior. His
brother-in-law Rodolfo was wholly a lost case. For a man like
Balcárcel, who made a devotion of labor and an idol of
wealth, the easy-going merchant who could accumulate nothing was an object of scorn. If to this were added Rodolfo's
social errors, he became the perfect target for Balcárcel's sermons, a kind of living text. The boy Jaime, as the son of such
a father, offered his uncle a double opportunity: on the one
hand, to make clear to him just how infirm were his father's
ethics, and on the other, to conduct him to better ways. Balcárcel did not love the boy, of course. He loved only Jorge
Balcárcel. But although the child irritated him, he also inter-
ested him as a kind of moral raw material. And he needed the
boy to make it possible for him to live in peace with his wife.

For this head of a family could not sire a family of his
own, and this was the crack in his imposing facade of manhood. The year of their marriage, the young couple had gone
to a doctor in London. "There is nothing wrong with you,"
the doctor said to Asunción. "You may have as many children

as you want." Jorge never told her the result of his own consultation. For several days he was strangely lost in thought. Then he buried himself in his studies and never mentioned the matter again. The months, the first years passed, and she never became pregnant. Her breeding did not allow her to discuss the matter with her husband, while he, on her menstrual days, affected silence and raised a wall of sternness that in time became one of his characteristics. Asunción's innocence, which in a normal relationship would have bloomed into normal sexuality, contracted and withdrew, and transformed itself into a concentrated, primitive internal violence. Sexual relations with her husband were purely mechanical. She lived in a world of unsatisfied appetites and broken hopes. She never discussed this with anyone. Only in dreams or in moments of solitude did she feed her visions of fecundity, and she would wake fatigued and hurry about her housework with drums echoing in her head and loins. Activity could distract her from her preoccupation, but she always returned to it.

When the Balcárcels came back to Guanajuato, Asunción observed her brother's marriage situation and formed her scheme. She urged Rodolfo to have a child. "It will bring true love into your life." She informed Adelina that her brother had indicated his displeasure at not having a son and heir, and then she suspected this was the cause of their present marital difficulties. Then, when Adelina confided that she was pregnant, Asunción made life so impossible for her that she fled the house. The last step was to arrange to separate the baby from the mother: a thousand pesos in *Don* Chepepón's hands, and it was done.

Her tormented dreams calmed. She filled her eyes, her lips, her hands with the infant's skin and soft smells and warmth. Her days were busy with maternal attentions, concern about his bath and diet and successive childhood illnesses. Her heart was alive with unforgettable hours: the boy's ABC's, their first lisped prayer together, Christmas mornings, his first tricycle, his first day at school, his first communion. She attended him with monomaniac love, and she sighed profoundly when she thought of the empty first years of her marriage. None of this escaped Balcárcel. He, like Asunción, understood that a great problem had been solved. The sterility which could have led to a permanent rancor between husband and wife, Jaime rendered harmless.

The first rule in this family was that life's real and important dramas should be concealed. Asunción had secretly plotted to gain a child, Rodolfo had secretly felt guilt for abandoning Adelina, but everything was hidden; the brother would never know that his sister had suffered in her sterility, the sister would never know that the brother accused himself —and her—of cruelty. Jorge Balcárcel was careless about the feelings of both. He gave, over and over, spoken rules and examples as to what in this or that situation should be done by people of good family, but his sayings were always abstract and the situations far from real. In their hearts all three of them understood and accepted that if one is not to be contradicted, one must not contradict, that if violence toward oneself is to be avoided, violence toward others must be eschewed. In a counterpoint of opaque silence and vague words, all clung to Jaime as the key to their contentment. Asunción's substitute son, the pretext for Balcárcel's authority, Rodolfo's link with the past, the child grew surrounded by love that had secret purposes and by standards that were Pharisaical.

"May he always be small, may he never grow up," the aunt would pray wordlessly every night. Then she would go to her nephew's room and observe him for several seconds, sleeping. She would draw near him and kiss his forehead, and close the curtains.

Chapter 3

H<small>IS MAMÁ SLEEPS</small> in the adjoining bedroom, the big room where prayers are held each evening and where there stands a beautiful piano that she sometimes—not often —plays. But his papá is not there with her. His papá lives far away on the roof, at the top of the winding iron outdoor stairs. That confuses the boy. Why don't his mamá and his papá live together? Why is his uncle where his father should be? And to which of them should he be more obedient: to stern Uncle Balcárcel, or to fat and drowsy Papá Rodolfo? Very early he learns the answer to that question: it is his uncle he must obey.

In his cloistered childhood solitude he explores the old mansion. The entrance is a green gate, very high and wide, that opens on the narrow street called Jardín Morelos. The corridor is broad, and ends at the patio, where there is a fountain. A palatial stone stairs rises on the right. On the wall above it, coats of arms are carved. A faded painting of the Crucifixion hangs on the landing, and when he is small, he stares up at the painting and crosses himself as if he were standing before the Virgin in Mamá Asunción's bedroom. Then the long drawing room, which in other times, when

Mamá Asunción and Papá Rodolfo were themselves children, was white and cheerful, with a floor of warm volcanic stone, and blonde walnut furniture. It was Grandfather Pepe who gave it its present thick drapes, maroon silk sofas, imitation marble columns, parquet floor, ornate chandeliers and green wallpaper. The drawing room has four balconies that look out upon the plaza of San Roque. A door of opaque glass with elaborate tracery leads to the musty closed dining room, beyond which, at the end of the wing, is the kitchen. A similar door hides the library, room of large black leather armchairs; and from the library he walks out onto the corridor that goes around and looks down upon the patio, green with plants and lichen.

A hall leads off at right angles and takes him to his aunt and uncle's room, then to his own. At the end of the hall is the bathroom. The tub is huge and the taps are of gold in the shape of lions' heads. The white porcelin has been stained by Guanajuato's rust-dyed brownish water.

On the left downstairs, just inside the entry, is an enormous room that he knows better than any other. It used to be the stable; now it is a catch-all storeroom. It is full of dust and cobwebs, old trunks and suitcases, discarded paintings, rickety furniture. A case, its glass cover broken, contains the mouldering butterfly collection which Mamá Asunción made as a young girl. Straw, darkened mirrors, old books that have lost their covers, forgotten sewing machines. A Tilbury without wheels. The black carriage upon which chickens roost. A wardrobe of moth-eaten clothes. An engraving of President Porfirio Díaz framed in blackened silver. An ancient dress dummy. High above, a skylight allows dusty gray light to enter.

This is his play place, the kingdom of his imagination. He opens boxes and trunks and makes games with their contents. He sits on the carriage seat and drives make-believe horses. He holds the old books between his hands and pretends to read even before he knows the alphabet. He visits the stable every day, clean and neat from his bath, and when he leaves it, he is covered with grime, which always earns him a scolding from Asunción.

Life is slow. The rooms are vast and he is small. The air is damp. There is something ruinous, decaying about it; at night it becomes so still, settling dust between the pleats of curtains that he fingers, tugs, and sometimes opens. The house is full of curtains. Green velvet conceals the main balconies. There is stiff brocade in the drawing rooms. Velvet again, red and stained, in Mamá Asunción's room. Cotton elsewhere. When the wind from the mountains comes, all these cloth arms lift and wave, topple over small tables, brush away bric-a-brac. It is as if heavy wings are trying to carry the house in flight. Then the wind ceases, the curtains are still, and the slow dust sifts again.

Life is calm. If there is rancor, it is hidden by respect for appearances. He never witnesses a quarrel, he never hears nor suspects a word of recrimination. The hours of the house are exact, affection is swift. The past is alive and close. Each time they take their places under the lamp in the dark dining room, memories are called up: some happy anecdote from Asunción, a homely one from Rodolfo, a story with a moral point from Uncle Balcárcel. He listens to the tinkle of glass and silver, and it is as if he were seeing his departed ancestors with his own eyes. A wonderful coming-out ball. A vacation in the country. A funeral. *Doña* Guillermina's profound prudence. *Don* Pepe's energy and gaiety. When Balcárcel pronounces that life in the old days was better in every way, Rodolfo and Asunción respectfully agree, and obedient Jaime does too. Balcárcel raises a finger and his voice: "Today morality is not what it was. Our obligation, decidedly, is to maintain those good old customs and to preserve respect for family in the midst of a society that is in serious crisis."

Following this summarizing statement, Asunción rings the

little silver bell and the servant comes in and takes away the plates. Rodolfo excuses himself and with slow steps leaves the dining room. They are all sleepy; it is siesta time. Their voices fade into silence. Doors are closed, curtains drawn. What silence those drowsy afternoons! The colonial city marks its hours with lost bells. From far-away fields comes the sound of grazing cattle. And in the silence of the siesta, just as at night, the boy is alone but does not feel alone. He is united with his family, both present and past, living and dead. He never wakes afraid of the dark.

At six he begins primary school. Revolutionary religious persecution has closed the church schools, and in the public ones, socialism is the official doctrine. He studies in a private home, the Senores Oliveros, along with most of the children of Guanajuato's rich Catholic gentry. At first a servant walks with him to the Oliveros, and comes for him in the afternoon when classes end. Soon he can go alone.

He has, instead of a briefcase, a little leather knapsack that straps on his back. Asunción takes care of it for him, puts into it the books and notebooks he will need today, sharpens his pencils, replaces erasers. She attends him devotedly at breakfast. She offers him sugared bread, more fruit, a glass of milk. Balcárcel observes and one morning remarks:

"You mama the child decidedly too much. Jaime, are you prepared for your arithmetic lesson?"

"Yes, Uncle."

"I was always the first in my class when I was your age, and I shall not tolerate my nephew to be second. Discipline in studies is the neccessary foundation for discipline in life. Are you afraid you will fail this year?"

"No, Uncle."

"Well, you ought to be. You should study for your examinations with the fear of a zero hanging over you. There is no other way to prepare conscientiously. The teacher always knows far more than his scholars, and he can fail the most studious."

"Yes, Uncle."

At seven he makes his First Communion, and his aunt begins to offer him religious readings: devotionals, missals, stories about the Virgin of Guadalupe, the Lives of the Saints. He goes with her, very early every morning, to Mass in the church of San Roque. At six every afternoon there are Rosary prayers in the big bedroom. Every Feast Day in the Church Calendar is celebrated, every Day of Obligation rigorously observed. Religion surrounds him until it becomes the very air he breathes.

The boy's faith is concrete and childish. As he studies catechism with Father Obregón, preparing for his First Communion, there are many words he does not understand. "Mass is the bloodless sacrifice of the law of grace." "The Church is Christ's spouse." He repeats and memorizes mechanically, these are mere words; for him Mass and the Church are the movements and gestures of the rich-robed priest before the golden altar, movements and gestures which he also memorizes and repeats in the secrecy of his bedroom. There, kneeling in front of the chair that is his improvised altar, he frowns and murmurs the prayers which begin Mass. He is afraid that he has forgotten some essential gesture or confused the order of the ritual: What comes next? Yes, the Introit and now the Kyrie Eleison. The Epistle. He does not speak aloud, he merely moves his mouth silently, for these words directed to everyone don't matter much: what is important is what he says to himself alone as he listens to the sermon. But the Credo he does say aloud: he knows it by heart. His hands fly about making the sign of the cross as he performs the Offertory of imaginary wine and bread. He washes his hands in his basin, kneels again; then the Canon and the Consecration; he lifts the cup of water high and whispers an Our Father. On his knees with his head bent he offers himself the ficticious communion. He remains there for several minutes with his eyes closed, and then gets up and empties the cup into the basin, and standing behind the chair, imparts benediction to his bed and dresser and washstand, while he pronounces the last words: "Ite, missa est." He cries them loudly, trying to imitate Father Lanzagorta's deep voice.

Thus God becomes his playmate, and the Church's sacred ritual a game. Usually he plays Mass in the afternoon. Sometimes, when he closes his curtains to make his room shadowy as San Roque, he sees children running down the alley. He knows them, they are his school-mates, they wave their arms to him, invite him to come out and play. The plaza fills with their shouts and laughter. And then Jaime feels sad. He cannot go out, it is forbidden. He shakes his head and tries to smile and stands at the window with his arms crossed on his chest. He feels lonely and isolated. And where is God? God has gone away. He bites his lips and asks himself why. Maybe he has failed to do something he ought to have done. Maybe, although he can't remember it, he has sinned terribly. This makes him sadder. If he has sinned, he must atone for his error. He grips a fold of the skin over his ribs and pinches and twists until the pain is sharp. That makes him feel a little better. He decides that he will go without his supper, as a deeper penitence. But Mamá Asunción will not allow that and forces him to eat until his plate is clean. And when he goes to bed, as always she comes in and leaves him a glass of milk and a square of quince candy.

As he lies there, he thinks of the Virgin, the Saints, the Holy Trinity, and God comes close to him again. But who is God? God is companionship and happiness. And Christ? He does not know Christ. He understands the Baby Jesus, yes, but the crucified Jesus, the figure who hangs upon a blood-smeared cross, is strange and terrible to him.

By the time he is eleven, he has decided that when he grows up, he will be a priest. He confides his ambition to

Asunción, expecting her to be pleased, but she at once looks troubled. A Ceballos a priest? There is something profoundly self-contradictory about that. Religion is an essential element in the life of a Ceballos, yes, just as is wealth. But Ceballos men are gentlemen and men of business, not Fathers. "You are just a little boy still," she tells Jaime. "You don't need to be thinking about what you will do when you grow up." Later she speaks with Balcárcel—the head of the family, the authority to whom problems must be brought for solution— and confesses that she is afraid the boy has taken his faith more seriously than is quite proper. Balcárcel grimly agrees, and one evening after dinner, summons him into the library.

Jaime sits in the armchair. He is sure that he has done something wrong and he trembles as he tries to think what it could be. Balcárcel paces back and forth tugging at his lapels. For a long time he says nothing, but his face is grave with displeasure. At last he speaks:

"You have a decidedly mistaken idea about religion. Religious training is certainly of the highest importance in life. Indeed it is indispensable: there is no other road to righteousness. But there can be too much of a good thing. Religious feeling carried to the extreme of mysticism is an absurdity." He stops and turns the full power of his cold stare upon the boy. "I observe such a tendency in you. It must be rooted out. Although Christian morality serves life, an unbalanced excess has no purpose whatsoever except to set you apart from the rest of mankind, endangering social relations which I assure you are just as important as good moral habits. I will not permit my nephew to make a fool of himself and be laughed at and pointed out as an idiot.

"When you go to your room, you will take down those ridiculous pictures of Virgins and saints with which you have plastered your walls. Out with them! Hereafter when you feel yourself full of piety, you will cross the plaza to the church and kneel in front of a real altar. And from tomorrow on, I forbid you to waste your leisure hours praying and reading Lives of Saints. Rather you will go out of doors and engage in physical exercise. Do I make myself clear?"

"Yes, Uncle."

"Then go, and let there be no more absurd talk about a religious vocation for you."

The boy leaves the library with bowed head. He approaches Asunción to be comforted, but she merely repeats, in soft words disguised as advice, the same cold orders.

Jaime obeys with a sense of injustice and resentment. The pictures tacked to the walls of his room come down. He no longer plays Mass. Dutifully he goes into the patio in the afternoon after school, and runs back and forth chasing a rubber ball. He obeys because that is his duty and he is a very dutiful child. But he feels that he has been hurt and misunderstood. Something that was really only a childhood game was given by his aunt and uncle a strange adult importance and implication which he does not understand. He feels confused. Apparently it is wrong to make God your companion. Apparently God is not for children but only for grown-ups. And you must not try to go to God directly and alone; you must cross the plaza and look for God in the Church. Those are the conclusions that he draws, but in his heart he refuses to accept them.

His feeling that his aunt and uncle have been unkind and unloving to him transforms itself into hostility that is expressed by withdrawing his affection from them. But he is a child and he wants to love and be loved. He turns toward the one person close to him who was not part of the injustice, who has never made him feel guilty or confused, the man who is as childlike as Jaime himself, his father.

Chapter 4

Rodolfo HAD CONTINUED to attend the store on San Diego. He made certain changes, chiefly the sale of ready-made suits. No longer did he offer the rich fabrics that had been featured in the old times when the social life of the city had been more select and the gap between the classes more accentuated. In those days the monk had been known by his habit; today, who could tell a gentleman from a chauffeur, when both dressed alike? Rodolfo made a speciality of cheap serge, gabardine, and cotton prints. He stopped importing cloth from Europe; that from Orizaba was cheaper and no one seemed to notice or care about the difference.

He tried to recover the lost ways of his careless youth, but under the sober respectability imposed by the Balcárcels, what had been open and pleasant became hidden and shameful. Dominoes, beer, the bordel, his pastimes were ruled by Asunción's rigid time-tables and the fear of meeting Balcárcel. Nor could he, with Adelina gone, adopt the pose of a serious man of family. He was trapped in an uncomfortable middle-ground between simplicity and inhibition, his plight sharpened by the Balcárcels' arid self-assurance.

Sometimes he thought about Adelina:

"Asunción, do you suppose she needs anything?"

"She's all right, don't worry about her. And for God's sake don't mention her in front of Jaime."

One morning in church he saw his wife at a distance and he felt ashamed and guilty. She had been thin before; now she was skeletal. More than once he would have willingly taken the boy to see her. But opportunities passed, he sought excuses, and he never had courage to steal Jaime away from Asunción's strict vigilance, much less enough to talk with him about his mother. Later he heard that *Don* Chepepón had died, and Adelina had left Guanajuato.

He was so accustomed to his son's distance from him that he received the boy's first advances toward intimacy hesitantly. He advised him, in a whisper, that the aunt and uncle had best not be told what they talked about together. He went secretly to the Oliveros house to bring Jaime home from school, so that they might have at least twenty minutes unobserved. Rodolfo's life took on clarity: he told himself that he must by all means gain Jaime's love. With unexpected imagination he made up stories, appealed to the child's curiosity, and absorbed his attention. Never in his life did Rodolfo know such happiness as that quick year, Jaime's twelfth. A new spirit came into his plump lazy body. With simple, natural eloquence he would relate events that he scarcely remembered, brightening their usual walk down Zapote to the foot of Jardín Morelos with a patina of anecdotes:

"Just imagine this very street jammed with carriages like the one in the stable. Your Great-grandmother Margarita surrounded by her children, saying hello to all the families that came to Mass on Sunday, and afterward taking chocolate with the *Señor* Bishop. It must have been beautiful, don't you think? And imagine, imagine, we had a little machine, something like a bike, to ride back into the past and to meet . . . even Pipila! Who was Pipila? Why, he was a little boy just like you, and it was thanks to him that the rebels took the Fort. Wouldn't you like to have known him? Some day we'll go to the Fort together, and I'll tell you . . ."

He was recompensed: the boy squeezed his hand, showered laughter and smiles upon him, gazed at him with clear eyes.

Father and son walked surrounded by crowds in the pilgrimage the Day of the Cave. They pushed forward through laughter and flowers on Friday of Sorrows. Hurrying, merry, impatient, they attended the gay ceremony of the opening of San Renovato Dam. Jaime devoured candy and shouted with glee when the gates were opened and the water rushed down while the band played "Over the Waves." He watched youths try to climb greased poles. He watched dancing, balloons, ferris wheels and merry-go-rounds. The crudely, brightly-painted world of fiesta made his eyes tremble and glow.

On one of their walks together, Jaime asked: "Tell me about the Revolution."

"It began in 1915," Rodolfo said. "I was at the hacienda and one fine day a gang of armed men rode up and emptied all the barns and burned some of the buildings. That same year the Carrancistas occupied Guanajuato and right away they made their headquarters in our house. Think of it: all those soldiers and their horses milling around in the patio, and your grandmother trembling with fear . . . and with good reason, too."

"And Mamá Asunción and Uncle Jorge?"

Rodolfo hesitated: "They had left Mexico."

"They left Grandmother Guillermina alone?"

"Yes, with Uncle Pánfilo, but . . . Well, they had just married, they were very young, life was so dangerous . . ."

"They left Grandmother alone?"

"She told them to go. They were so young and they felt they had a right to see something besides massacre and sacking. They . . . I don't know."

"I would like to have known Grandmother Guillermina."

"And of course they couldn't take her with them. Wild horses wouldn't have dragged her away from her home!" He smiled.

"They left her. I would have stayed with her. Why didn't they?"

"Eh! How you ask questions! Today you're not even looking where you're walking, all you can do is ask questions. That's enough now. We'll go to the lake, and . . ."

"If we have another Revolution, I won't leave you alone."

"I know you won't. Don't think any more about it. Your grandmother was a very strong-willed woman, and your aunt and uncle . . . that is, *Don* Jorge and your Mamá Asunción . . . well, they were young and they had a right to a better life than was possible here then. And . . ."

The boy squeezed his father's hand and was silent.

Holy Friday. He was thirteen now. They were watching the Three Falls at the Compañía Church. Tiny below the great high dome, squeezed against the rose-colored wall by the press of the crowd, the boy nailed his eyes on the figure of Christ, the wild bristly black hair, the thorn scratched forehead. Suddenly he found himself understanding for the first time that what his Uncle Balcárcel said was not true. He was sure that the Man represented by that sad image had never been unbalanced; but Uncle Balcárcel, if he had known Him, would certainly have called Him so.

His feeling deepened. He could not have expressed it in words, it was too fluid, too warm, too overpowering. The Cross advanced slowly and irresistibly carried upon the powerful arms of brown ragged Indians. Hands stretched trying to touch it: concentrated life enamated like heat. It was as if the Indians were trying to lose themselves in touching the image. It was as if they wanted their faith not to give them something, but to lead them to renunciation. Their piety was not a way of life but a road out of life. They wanted to lose themselves in the anonymity of this moment, giving up everything past and future.

Carried high, the black-skinned Jesus was Lord of them all, but not with hope. The Indian's peasant faces showed a secret desire to go back and seize what had once been possessed and then lost. There was also a challenge. Only Indians held the image; creoles and meztizos remained on the sidewalks, on balconies, looking on with an air of condescension, as if they were receiving what had been specially brought for them. And this in a mysterious way exalted the faith and confidence of the men whose arms carried the Cross. This was really *their* fiesta; today they were the protagonists and, united with the venerated image, the center of the ceremony. Silently they clamored their triumph.

Jaime watched and felt something new. The intense pigments of the fiesta clouded his thought, but suddenly, behind the glitter and the crowd, something formed that joined him to the image on the Cross. The people and the noise went away and he and Christ were facing each other, alone together.

Then his uncle's words echoed saying that mortality was identical for everyone, that the rules of Christian conduct were the same for all, for women as for men, for children as for adults, for the poor as for the rich; it made no difference what a man was himself and alone. And now Christ and Jaime Ceballos were no longer soul to soul; Christ had returned to the multitude. Squeezed against the wall by the crowd, Jaime burned to recapture that look that had been only for him, that no one else could see or understand.

A purple cowl fell over the dark image. The crowd dispersed.

Jaime went to the church every day the following week to see if the cowl had been removed. He felt deeply that the figure of Christ held a secret reserved only for him. His prayers that week were an effort to learn the secret.

Good Friday he walked with his father in the procession. He realized later that it was then, staring again at the image of the victimized God, that he had for the first time felt himself a person, an individual, different not only from everyone in his family but from everyone in the world. During the frugal dinner that evening—evening of mourning underlined by the dark clothing his father and aunt and uncle wore— he observed his father flush when Balcárcel intoned his customary words about the family and good breeding. Jaime did not listen to the conversation. He thought only of Christ; he raised his eyes to the lamp and imagined that he saw the bleeding Body there, the crown of thorns. That night he dreamed of death, for the first time with terror. With the bed-covers pulled up to his ears, he dreamed about his dead ancestors: Higinio Ceballos with open mouth and hands crossed upon his still chest; Margarita Machado with a lace coif; Pepe Ceballos like a wax doll, and Grandmother Guillermina with a handkerchief tied around her jaw. His dead ancestors smiled at him; they were like him or they were part of him, they were friendly and comforting. Then, unexpectedly, from the vague background, appeared a strange figure who shattered all tranquility, the corpse who had died in pain and blood, a horrible corpse who between his nail-pierced hands bore a mysterious offering that in the dream could neither be seen nor understood. The figure grew larger and larger with a bellowing sound and crushed Jaime's ancestors; their bodies fell broken and grotesquely smiling at his feet; a storm of lights whirled and everything dissolved, and Jaime woke screaming. He raised his hands to his mouth. His aunt ran in, barefoot and wrapped in a shawl, to calm him and make the sign of the cross over him.

Then it was morning: Holy Saturday. He woke with the

THE GOOD CONSCIENCE   [41

memory of his dream, to the bang of exploding rockets. He knew what the day would be like. The whole family would attend religious ceremonies. The purple garments would fall from the images. The Virgin would smile again, the saints blaze in cloth-of-gold. Incense would fill the naves. When he got up and went into the bathroom for his bath, he thought happily about the promised spectacle. He passed the wash-cloth over his shoulders and felt them stronger and broader than they had been even yesterday. The tub was brim-full of rust-colored hot water. He stirred his legs and stretched his feet until he touched the gold taps; not long ago, he had not been able to do that. Water splashed his armpits with a good feeling. He soaped himself and went on thinking about this day of celebration. Already rockets were soaring and boys were running carrying papier-maché bullsheads. Already glory was clanging from all the bell-towers in the city. Judas dolls with red noses and black mustaches would explode. They would all walk to church: his father, his aunt, himself—not Uncle Balcárcel, who would be absent from Guanajuato today. They would join the crowd to celebrate the Resurrection; they would kneel in front of the confessionals, they would open their lips to receive the Host, while the chorus raised the Easter halleluja. Then again outside the church, walking slowly, surrounded by noise and happiness. The soap slipped away and Jaime, looking for it, ran his hands down his legs, which had begun to be hairy. When he got out of the tub, he stood before the mirror for a long time, wrapped in a towel, studying his face.

There was faith in the city of noble stone that Saturday. Peasants came down from the barren hills. Shepherds walked in from San Miguel with jingling bells on their ankles and wrists. Old folks crowded balconies. Children ran through the mass of *rebozos* and straw hats. On every corner in Guanajuato there was a water-vendor's stand or a fruit-stand or a flower-stand. From the rococco distance of the Valenciana the smell of exploding firecrackers came. The city smelled of gunpowder, but also of manure, of damp paving stones, of trees. Many odors rose from the earth, others from vendors, others from sideboards and cupboards behind whose white doors were fresh cheeses, rice with milk, sticky candies, bunches of cherries, eggnog, fruit wine, guava and march-pane. All these scents were in the air that Holy Saturday, for this was a provincial city of pastries and cordials more inter-ested in the elaborate adornment of a nougat or an altar than in the efficiency of a liquidizer. And surrounded by these scents the people of Guanajuato gathered in the wide plazas to celebrate the great Christian holiday.

A holiday greater, perhaps, than Bethlehem night. For it was now that the reward promised by Christmas would be collected. The Savior had died for all, and upon rising from that common death, had promised all salvation from pain and solitude saying that to live for one's brothers, as He had died, is to secure eternal life. He who knew how to love his brothers could live in them forever, and in their children, and their children's children. Because this had been promised, Asunción Balcárcel walked down the hill to the church of the Compañía, holding Jaime, still a child to her, by the hand. Because of the promise, the merchant Rodolfo Ceballos trod heavily behind his sister and his son, in his black suit, with his hands piously folded over his chest. And because of the promise, the chorus of boys was singing Handel's Halleluja when the family entered the church and took their usual seats among the gentry, and the voices that sang Mass were joyful, and Easter candles were blessed, and at the end the *Exsultet* was cried.

Jaime remained on his knees. He was wearing his blue Sun-day suit and it had become too small for him, and the seams of the trousers had split when he knelt. Beside him his aunt was reading her missal. Rodolfo's mouth was half open and his gaze was lost in the baroque foliage of the altar. Jaime had eyes for only the enormous candle. He was reflecting, with surprise, that he had attended Holy Saturday ceremonies all his life without ever realizing that that candle was the center of everything, and the whole object was to light it. He understood now and felt full of happiness as he watched big drops of wax melt down and the high flame slowly flatten. The candle was sacrificing itself giving off rejoicing light. Asunción's voice repeated beside him: ". . . and in the resurrection of the body, and life everlasting, Amen."

They rose, crossed themselves before turning away from the altar, and with difficulty pushed out into the jam-packed aisle. Asunción's body squeezed against him. The little bells of the acolytes tinkled. It was impossible to advance, almost impossible to breathe. And Asunción's body pressed against him harder and harder until his goose-pimpling flesh could feel the round softness of her breasts and belly. He turned his head. She lowered hers. At last they reached the noisy exit, the cry of vendors, the chirping of birds, the warm mild scents of the provincial city, the dance of flute-players and Indian feathers that pranced around the plaza.

That evening the three of them were alone in the house: Balcárcel had departed in the morning for Mexico City to—as he said—attend to some business that had been postponed because of Holy Week. The forty days of silence had ended, and Asunción, recalling how *Don* Pepe used to have a little chamber orchestra come play Holy Saturdays after dinner, said that she wanted to hear music. Rodolfo and Jaime accompanied her to the bedroom of red velvet curtains and she seated herself before the piano that had been given her as a child. She played, with occasional indecisions. *Für Elise.* Rodolfo sat on a cane chair with his fat body slumped and his head hanging forward, absorbed in memories. The last of afternoon filtered through the window. Jaime stood near it, his profile silhouetted and his hair fired by the low sun.

"Mamá's favorite piece," said Asunción, repeating the opening of the work.

Rodolfo nodded.

"Papá gave me this piano. Do you remember?"

"Yes. When you were ten."

"We used to have a grand piano, too. It was in the drawing room. You know, I'd forgotten about it. Whatever happened to it?"

"Yes," said Rodolfo, sighing. "*She* sold it."

"If we hadn't come back from England, she would have sold the whole house. It's a miracle anything was left."

"Well . . . she didn't know how to play. And just then the victrola was the great novelty . . ."

Asunción lifted her hands from the cold keys and with her head indicated that Jaime was listening. Languid as the sun, the boy stood with one hand on the curtain. *She, she, she.* He put the word away without thinking about it. With a sense of strangeness he reflected that today much was happening that he did not understand. Someday he would. "Someday I'll understand everything," he told himself, and he swiftly thought about the church, the ceremony of light and sacrifice, his aunt's still young body pressed against his own. He released the curtain and with a slow step left the room.

"The point is, she wasn't like us," Asunción said louder. She began to play Chopin's *Impromptu,* but she didn't remember it well and had to open the score. Jaime drifted down the hall. "Are you trying to upset him?" she said as she narrowed her eyes to read the notes. "Remember what the Bible says."

"But she's his mother."

"No, she isn't, Rodolfo," Asunción smiled acidly as her brother assumed the look of a victim. "The boy has no mother. I'm not going to let you corrupt him."

"He will have to meet her sooner or later."

"He will *not!* If you insist, I'm going to have my husband talk with you."

Rodolfo wanted to ignore the threat. He wanted to speak in general terms. He couldn't go on.

"Adelina is in Irapuato living very contentedly now," said his sister. "She has the lowest sort of friends, people just like herself. She ought never to have tried to leave them. A woman who doesn't know her place is . . ."

"Stop. Please don't say anything else. Maybe you're right. But try to understand me. I . . . I feel ashamed of myself. Yes. If I had let her see the boy just once . . . or if we had helped her somehow."

"Don't be silly. She gave the child up quite willingly, didn't she, so that her father could have a few more pesos."

"*Don* Chepepón is dead now. She has a hard time."

"She's better off than ever."

"I don't understand you. You talk as if she were evil. She was never evil, Asunción."

Night had fallen. The room filled with shadow. Rodolfo was thinking that his sister had known very well what had happened to the grand piano. She watched everything, she noticed everything, nothing could be hidden from her.

Asunción closed the score of the *Impromptu* and returned to *Für Elise*, which she had by memory.

"Enough. I advise you not to say anything about this to my husband, he will hardly be pleased to discuss it. And no more between you and me, either."

The gray cat came to Asunción's feet and began to purr, arching with pleasure.

Easter Sunday. Jaime, just back from Mass, comes out the green gate and sits down on the steps with an orange in his hand. He stretches his legs along the hot stone, sucks warm juice, and watches the street. Churchgoers pass on their way to spend the day in the ecclesiastical darkness of San Roque.

Servant girls with lettuce and celery wrapped in their *rebozos*. Girls with long hair and budding breasts who giggle and whisper hand-in-hand. Barefoot children who spread their ripe black avocado eyes and race along the street click-clacking window bars with a stick. Beggars, most of them old, some of them blind, a few crippled adolescents, who display an opaque eye, a bloody sore, a nervous spasm, a twisted foot, a paralyzed tongue: they move down the proud street with their faces turned up to the sky, some of them crawling on hands and knees, others pushing themselves along on little wooden platforms with roller-skate wheels.

Humanity. It squeezes through the narrow alleys and spreads out into the plaza, swirls for a moment, and sweeps on, squeezed compact again, through new alleys. There are few Indians. Faces are burned leather Meztizo, deep with wrinkles, eyes green and greasy in olive flesh. Hair is black and lustrous, or white-blue like a dawn volcano.

An Indian woman with hips high under her heavy skirt stops at the corner, opens her mouth of narrow teeth, stretches a scrap of canvas shadow upon three wooden staffs. She spreads her wares on the paving stones: pineapple and slices of watermelon, perfumed quinces, opened pomegranates, mamey fruit, little lemons, *jícama,* green oranges, limes, *zapotes,* mulberries and pancake-like cactus leaves.

A strawberry vendor chants.

Long candles hang their reposing virility beneath the tarp of the vendor of lithographs of the Virgin and silver hearts.

Baskets of flowers that go by making their carriers hump-backed: daisies and jasmine, roses and blue dahlias, lilies, drowsy poppies, solemn canna lilies and playful carnations; they leave the brief wake of their scents the length of the street.

The gray cat comes out the gate rolling like a ball of yarn, and Jaime smiles. Boy and cat rub each other. The yellow eyes open and the cat returns to hide in the shadow of the house.

A scissors-sharpener rests his wheeled shop and pumps his foot-pedal and makes knives and scissors and razors glitter in the powerful sun.

A damp-flanked mule laden with cut sugar cane moves from door to door.

A *charro* rides erect in his saddle leading a group of pinto horses. One of the horses stops and rises on its hind feet and tries to mount the cane vendor's mule. The *charro* dismounts and quirts the flanks of the stallion until it finally rejoins the group of pintos. A hoof knocks over the Indian woman's tower of oranges and she silently rebuilds it while beggars from the church scramble after the oranges that roll away, like tiny suns, across the cobblestones.

Jaime touches the single hair that has sprouted on his chin and watches the horses grow distant and the shouting of the *charro* become faint. He spits out seeds. Humming, he enters the *zaguan* and turns into the old stable. He wipes his hands on his thighs and climbs up on the dusty driver's seat of the black carriage. He clucks his tongue and snaps an invisible whip over an imaginary team. The air in the stable is dusty and dry, but the boy's nostrils are full of the smells of horses' sweat, horses' excrement, the hot sexuality of the stallion when it drew near the quiet croup and red anus of the mule. His eyes are closed, but they still see the street and bathe in its colors. His clenched hands, stretched toward make-believe, almost touch the flesh of the crippled beggars, the melting wax of the white candles, the high buttocks of the Indian woman, the little breasts of the young girls: the world that is born soon, lives soon, dies soon.

He drops the imaginary reins and unbuttons the fly of his pants and puts his hands to his genitals, feels the downy hair that has recently appeared there. He does not know how to say it, as he trembles high on the coachman's seat with his pants open and his hand curled around his stiffening penis; he does not know how to say how much he loves everything, the rich flowing life he has just watched, the fruit and the flowers and the animals and the people. But now it is all gone. The horses have clattered out of sight. The Indian woman has gathered up her fruit and taken down her scrap of canvas and departed. The flowers have gone, shunning him like the girls who would not look toward him. And he wanted so much for everything to stay that he could love it, touch it, hold it close. He sees himself with his thin face and his blond hair, his shirt open and his sleeves rolled, his feet extended beside the hot street; he has not moved, but the whole world has: it has fled from his eyes and hands and escaped him. "What doesn't go away?" he asks himself. "What never goes away but waits forever still and full of love?" He buttons his pants with difficulty and jumps down from the carriage feeling a sharp pain in his testicles.

He runs out on the street and climbs the hill, sweating. The high dome of the Compañía church, lord of the land-scape, is his guide. He runs so hard that his feet burn and his tendons ache. The church is empty, services have ended. Beside the central nave stands the knotted Cross of sacrifice upon which hangs the black Christ. He stops in front of it. It is not fear but love that holds him motionless, the same inexplicable love he felt in the stable remembering the morning. Christ's earth-colored face looks down, furrowed with blood. The metal eyes shine beneath the brows of painted torment. The wounded body does not move, though the arms are alive crying pain and welcome. The brief skirt, bordered with jewels, hangs stiff over the belly and down to the knees, and below it descend the lacerated rivers of the legs to their meeting in the single nail that pierces the feet. Jaime is sure that the body of the Savior will not go away, will not escape him as the world did. He kneels. Slowly he opens his pants again, and begins to masturbate. The church is silent, there is only the whispering of candles that flicker on both sides of the image. A strange tingling that he has never known before rises from his hot loins. He grips the crucified feet.

Silence overcomes silence. Something—the wax drippings of the candles—measures time again. The ecstasy of his orgasm passes and he lifts his eyes to the figure and does not know whether his body is Christ's, or Christ's is his. He turns and looks around the church. Then he stands and draws near the image and raises the stiff skirt. The reproduction of nature ends at the knees: the rest is a plain wooden cross which supports the wounded torso and the open arms.

"Not one word, kid, or I'll break your back . . ."

He had returned from the empty church along empty streets. It was afternoon. Everyone was sleeping, the meal ending Lent had been abundant, Guanajuato's belly was heavy, even the domes of the churches seemed drowsy. He had walked home slowly. Where were the street vendors, the *charro*, the young girls? After his experience in front of the image of Christ, he would have liked to see them again: maybe—he thought—they would notice him now. The girls would look at him. The *charro* would ask him to help take the pintos to their stable. The Indian woman would offer him a slice of *jicama*. For now he was different. "I must be different. My face must be changed. They won't see me the same. At dinner tonight I'll watch how they stare at me. Am I a man now? But all the boys at school have done it and they look the same as before. Maybe no one will notice anything." He observed, a little fearfully, his reflection in windows. "Everyone is sleeping. Sunday siesta. I must be the only person in the city who is awake." The colonial town in its solitude was like a great gold coin.

He did not want to go upstairs. "I don't want a siesta. It's that I don't want to see them, that's all. I'll go and see

what I can find in the trunk." He pushed open the squeaky
stable door and then a hand closed over his mouth and a
knee was in his back.

"Not one word, kid . . ."

There was a stench of sweat that did not smell of filth nor
of labor; it was a different kind of sweat. It wiped away the
odors of the morning: flowers, fruit, candles, horses, leather,
washed hair. The hand held his lips still and the knee pushed
him toward the back of the room, between the trunks and
the dress dummies, behind the old carriage.

Then the hand released him and at the same time pressed
the point of an iron bar against his chest. "Just take it easy."
Jaime was too confused to see clearly. He was aware of
someone powerful and shadowy and threatening, and he
thought of a thief, an escaped criminal. Then his eyes focused
and he saw the man. Tall, strong, black hair falling over his
forehead, eyes that were not those of a thief or a criminal.

They stared at each other.

Jaime panted and wiped his nose on his arm. The man
was motionless except for his eyes, which moved from side
to side not with fear but with dominating confidence. There
was a pimple on his lip. His shoes, crude laborer's brogans,
were scarred and dusty. His blue shirt was dry but bore the
stains of sweat. The cuffs of his pants were rolled up. If his
chest and shoulders were powerful, his legs were as thin as
wires.

"Listen to me now. I'm hungry and very thirsty. You are
going to go inside and bring me food and water. Do you
understand? You aren't going to tell anyone that I'm here.
Stop looking so scared. Go on, now, and remember what
happens to squealers. Hurry."

Now serene, now threatening, his voice seemed to come
near and then drift far away.

"Go on, do what I tell you."

Jaime was immobile in the corner.

"Look, kid, I'm about to fall over from lack of sleep and hunger."

Jaime stepped forward and touched the man's hand and ran out.

A few minutes later he returned carrying a laden napkin, and the stranger smiled. He took the napkin and spread it open on the trunk. Slices of ham and cheese, chicken wings, a cube of quince candy.

"Here is the pitcher, *Señor*."

"Call me Ezequiel."

"All right, *Señor* Ezequiel."

The man put down a chicken wing and laughed: "Just plain Ezequiel. How old are you?"

"Thirteen. Going on fourteen."

"Do you work?"

"No. I belong to the family. I go to school."

They seated themselves on the trunk of memories in which reposed *Doña* Guillermina's veils and magazines of the last century. Ezequiel chewed furiously, smearing the droopy mustache with grease. Again and again he pounded Jaime's knee; he could not hold in his happiness, as robust as his thick chest and the dark eyes that moved continually from the boy to the door to the skylight. *You learn something in this god-damn fight and that's how to tell who is for you and who isn't. Who is this kid? Just a little sissy, I thought when I saw him. A servant in this rich home, when he went for the food. He has helped me. No, I don't know. A lonely kid, that's all.*

"What's your name?"

"Jaime."

"Good. Take some of this candy, Jaime. Go on, don't be bashful. Do I have to twist your arm?"

"Thank you, *Señor* Ezequiel."

"None of that *señor* business, I told you."

"Ezequiel."

"Well, what did you think when I grabbed you? You thought I was a crook, didn't you?"

"Yes."

"Do you have many friends?"

"No."

"I was sure of that! Here, take some water. You don't know what it's like to taste fresh water after three days walking across the desert and hiding in freight cars. Did you ever hear anyone talk about Ezequiel Zuno?"

"No. But that's you."

"Sure, it's me." *Maybe he won't understand me. I better keep my mouth shut. But I haven't spoken to a living soul for days. Sometimes I even had hallucinations. There's nothing worse than the high desert, you're too close to the sun. And you get mad because you know it isn't a real desert but just land that won't hold water any more because it has been misused. When I dropped off the freight, the land was still like bone.* "You don't have any idea how good I felt when I slipped into Guanajuato last night and came to the lake."

"What?"

"Nothing, nothing. I'm worn out. I'm so tired I don't know what I'm saying. I'm going to lie down. Will anyone come in here?"

"No. But if you want, I'll stay."

"They won't look for you?"

"My uncle . . . *Señor* Balcárcel . . . is in Mexico City. They won't look for me until dinner time."

"Good. Afterward, I'll tell you a story. But now . . ." *There's no reason to tell him anything. He doesn't have to know what it is when they beat you . . . he doesn't have to know what names they call you, or what it's like to have to hang on and take it, afraid that at any moment you'll give in to them . . . he doesn't have to know how you get to feel-*

*ing that to give in would be so easy, while to hang on and
spit back at them is hard.*

He fell asleep, his legs spread, his head against the trunk.
He dreamed of men in long files. It was his recurring dream,
but he never remembered it. When he woke, the boy was
still there, sitting on the floor staring at a butterfly case
with a shattered cover.

Like a faithful pup. My little sentry.

"Are you rested now, Ezequiel?"

"Yes, *mano.* Thanks for staying."

Decaying light from the skylight fell on his oily eyelids.

"What time is it, Jaime?"

"About six."

"Let me have that pitcher again. Ah!"

He rubbed his eyes and stretched.

"Couldn't you sleep on the freight train?"

"Cat-naps. Not real sleep, what with the heat and the stink
of cattle."

"Why, Ezequiel?"

"Why what? Why am I running and hiding? Probably because I'm a fool. Sure, why does a man do anything? You
could let things ride so easily. You have your wife and kids
. . . God knows how they're getting along now! Sure, sure.
But you aren't alone. That's the problem, no one is alone.
And when they haul you in front of the *cacique* and you
beg him to let the men in the mine organize, and you even
manage to get them all together outside the rathole shaft and
put on a demonstration . . . well, then you know it isn't just
yourself but all the others too. You say to hell with your family and your little job in the open air on top of the ground,
and you gamble everything. That's what happened."

The light disappeared from the skylight, but the copper
rivets in Zuno's belt still shone. Jaime felt that that guttural
voice came from the stomach, that Ezequiel pressed a copper
button and made the voice speak.

"But why am I telling you? The silicosis and the men who are killed and the others who are so sick by the time they're thirty that all they can do is crawl through abandoned veins scraping together a few kilos of rock that they have to sell at any price they can get. Then, when you finally organize them all and take them out one night, carrying lanterns, to march in front of the administration building, something that had never happened before because we were supposed to be so stupid and yellow . . . But I talked with them, to each man alone and to all of them together, telling them to unite so we could get what was ours. The gringos didn't even come outside. They just sicked the *cacique* on me. I was locked up in jail and they beat the hell out of me trying to make me order the boys back to work. But I knew that trick. Once I called the strike off, they'd have shot me. That's why I escaped, kid. So I can go back still alive and kicking at them. So I can find other men like me, and working all together . . ."

"*Jaime!*"

Doña Asunción's voice floated down the stone stairs. The boy, seated at Ezequiel's feet, jumped but did not get up.

"What are you going to do, Ezequiel?"

"I have to get to Guadalajara. I've friends there. You run along now. In the morning, bring me some breakfast."

"When will you leave?"

"Tomorrow night. I'll rest here one day, and then push on."

"Let me help you," said the boy, taking the miner's hands.

"You've helped me already."

"*Jaime! Jaime!*"

"Now run on before they suspect something."

"I'll see you in the morning before I go to school."

"Sure. Thank's for everything. Run now."

Ezequiel Zuno stretched his legs again. He crossed his arms behind his head and breathed the stables' accumulated decay. *That's my kid. And just a few hours ago he thought he was alone in the world too.*

Jaime climbed the lordly stairs with a new step. The things of the world would not escape him again, they were fixed now. He saw Christ very close, hanging upon nails. Ezequiel Zuno still closer, and not mute like the crucified figure. The Easter candle which was lit in order to be consumed. His own adolescent body, half-boy, half-man, the body he had discovered today, which joined them all, Christ, Ezequiel, and the candle. As he went up the stairs he touched his face, his shoulders, and his thighs. On the landing, the varnished colors of the Crucifixion opened like a fan. And above, at the head of the stairs, waited the impatient dark-clad woman.

"Look at your face! What have you been doing, rolling in the dust? May Jesus save me! Your uncle is coming. Go change your clothes. Hurry."

There is something uneasy about this boy, Licenciado Jorge Balcárcel reflected as he finished breakfast and wiped his lips with his napkin. He is trying to fool us. He may fool the others, but not me.

Jaime had not been listening to the conversation and when Balcárcel addressed him, he flushed.

"You are decidedly absent-minded. Don't you have to go to school today? Holidays seem merely to weaken your will. Come, come, boy!"

His face has changed, the uncle thought on. He is beginning to be a man. A pimple on his forehead. An adolescent now, who will be like all the others, undisciplined, insolent to his elders, obsessed with women. Well, I'll handle him! He'll want to smoke, drink, go to whore houses. Naturally he will be rebellious. Pimples. Shaving. Then disobedience, but we'll see about that.

"Quick! I'm not joking."

Drowsily Jaime rose and pushed his chair back and excused himself. He finished his glass of *café con leche* standing in front of his uncle's frown. He picked up his school knapsack and walked toward the kitchen.

"Here there! What business do you have in the kitchen?"

"A glass of water."

"Isn't there water on the table?"

He believes that he has me fooled. That knapsack is stuffed with something. He is taking food to the parish beggars. When did this generosity begin?

"Excuse me. I didn't notice."

"You didn't notice. Someday you won't notice the hole you fall into. Get along now, and watch the way you answer back to me."

"I said excuse me."

"And I said off to school! Insolent! You'll have no allowance this week, and that may not be the worst."

Jaime crossed the drawing room and went down the stairs. At the stable door he rapped softly. There was no reply. He held his breath and opened the door. He ran, nervously, to the far end.

"So it's you, kid!"

"Ezequiel! I thought you had gone! How do you feel?"

"Better. I'm leaving tonight. Did you bring me something to eat?"

"Here, take it. They nearly caught me."

"They don't suspect anything?"

"No."

"Will you be back at noon?"

"Yes. I'll see you again."

"No, they may catch you. Better say goodbye now."

"No! Let me come back!"

Ezequiel rubbed the boy's head.

"What a baby you are. If you really want to help me, don't come. I will leave when it gets dark."

The strength of a real man, Jaime thought. There was nothing about him that was like Uncle Balcárcel. He stared at Ezequiel wordlessly. He wanted to remember him, never forget him.

"Shake hands, Jaime, and thanks for understanding and helping me."

They clasped hands.

"Ezequiel, when will I see you again?"

"All of a sudden some day you don't expect to."

"Are you going to win?"

"Sure as the sun rises."

"Will you let me help you again then . . . I mean, when you've won and I've grown up?"

Zuno smiled and slapped the boy's shoulder.

"Sure. But you're already almost grown. You've proved it. Now slip out, we don't want them suspecting anything."

Jaime reached the door and turned.

"I'm your friend, Ezequiel. Don't forget me."

Ezequiel answered with a finger to his lips:

"Shhhhh!"

Uncle Balcárcel hid in the patio and watched the boy come out of the stable. He cracked his knuckles.

"Look, boys!"

"A prisoner!"

"With soldiers guarding him!"

"He must be a bandit!"

They crowded across the school yard. The bell ending recreation period rang and the prefects began to shout:

"Line up! Line up!"

Four soldiers were leading a man whose wrists were bound.

"Look what a face he has!"

On tiptoes, Jaime watched them pass. With a drowned gasp and his legs and arms pounding he ran out the gate and down the narrow street of sunlight and shadow until he reached the five silent marching men.

"Ezequiel!"

His cry was not of anguish. It was of guilt, self-accusation. Zuno walked with his eyes fixed on the paving stones. Sweat had broken out on his forehead and across his back. His heavy miner's shoes clattered. The bayonets of the four soldiers flashed light across his face.

"Ezequiel! It wasn't me! I swear, it wasn't me!"

Jaime ran in front of them, running backward, facing them. The street dipped abruptly, and he lost his footing. They passed beside and above him.

"It wasn't me! I'm your friend!"

The boots marched on. A few curious passersby stared down at the boy lying on the stones.

"It wasn't me . . ."

Chapter 5

Each year of life, like a night's repose, has depths of profound dream and summits of wakefulness. Life in a provincial capital, once experienced, tends to drain off into shadows. In memory whole hours and days are lost. Only isolated scenes remain, persisting because they have burrowed deep and put out roots. Fourteen years: the Bible for his birthday. Fifteen years: the voices of those who have an opinion about him, who make remarks about him, who feel themselves responsible for his future, who point the road he should take. Priests who sip chocolate with *Doña* Asunción. Stiff ladies who come calling. Mild-eyed *señoritas* who already are Daughters of Mary. Politicians and businessmen who breakfast with Uncle Balcárcel. He had wanted people, he had sought a voice in a wooden statue varnished with blood, and he had believed that the only human voice was that of the miner, Ezequiel Zuno. Now the tongues of a hundred gratuitous preceptors may be heard, all friends in the immediate world of his aunt and uncle, and the boy must perforce listen. *Don* Tereso Chávez, director of his school, who has faith in Jaime and also halitosis. Father Lanzagorta, *Doña* Asunción's confessor, who barks his Sunday sermons and every Friday hungrily presents his greyhound profile at dinner. *Señor* Eusebio Martínez, leader of the Party of the Mexican Revolution, who wishes *Licenciado* Balcárcel to become patron of a Youth Front for the approaching presidential elections. *Doña* Presentación Obregón, public relations officer for the Trinity, who promotes Holy Week retreats, apostolic congregations, novenas for every defunct celebrity, exercises of the Corpus, prayers in private homes, the procession on the day of the Virgin of Guadalupe, the blessing of animals. *Don* Chema Naranjo, Balcárcel's competitor in buying lots and making loans for short terms at high interest. *Don* Norberto Galindo, old Villista, who switched to Ogregón following the battle of Celaya, and through cattle-theft has become a substantial rancher. *Señorita* Pascualina Barona, efficient moral edile, watchful in movies, at dances, even on the streets in the small hours of the morning, to catch serenaders, hands-holding, those who come home late: gold *pince-nez* and a small black bonnet. The ex-legislator Maximino Mateos, who bosses three small towns and operates a complex tax system the returns from which he invests through Balcárcel. J. Guadalupe Montañez, a cousin, one of the last examples of the old regime.

They all visit the stone mansion. They all speak. Jaime writes beautiful compositions. Sometimes he must read them aloud three times. What original ideas the boy has! Clearly there is a certain want of finish in style. I will lend him—with your permission—a volume of *Don* Amado Nervo, whose literary excellence is beyond dispute.

Encourage him toward a religious vocation, *Doña* Asunción. I'm told that he recites whole chapters of Scripture from memory. Good. But let him be sure, if he decides upon priesthood, to stand solid as an oak, capable of resisting all temptation. So many seminarians abandon their habits after only one year! The Church has need of new buds. St. Peter's tree has been shattered by too many impious bolts of lightning.

There are so many towns that have no priest. It didn't used to be so, and Holy Mary's favorite people deserve something better.

—Yes, this will be the first really civil government since Madero. An administration of university graduates and young men. Say the word, and with luck your nephew may rise to be deputy. The Party is going to build in accordance with the new historical circumstances of the Revolution, and now we civilians will feed with a large spoon. We need youth, sir, and also businessmen like yourself, to fight against the Padillista reaction. I assure you that we are finished with the red demagogues of my General Cárdenas . . . though he himself is of course a disciplined member of the Party who knows how to respect the nation's highest interests. I urge you to help in forming the Youth Front. Bring me your nephew, he too must become a cub of the Revolution.

—We'll meet at my home the day of the Holy Cross. I've already had the prayers printed. Bring the boy, too, of course. From the house we will march in procession to the church of San Diego, and afterward we'll have refreshments in the sacristy. Last year it was difficult. Some ex-governor or other wanted to raise a riot with the Constitution. So many communist governors, my dear, but they all leave office millionaires. May God protect us!

—Maximino Mateos' son is an ass but for all that his paper is sound. I've raised interest on him to forty percent a week, and he still borrows. I tell you because he may come to you: forty percent, no less. How is your nephew coming along? Teach him to be saving and prudent, *Don* Jorge. What if he should turn out a prodigal like the son of Maximino Mateos?

—When your nephew finishes his secondary studies, let that be enough of books. Send him to my ranch, and there he will grow into a strong and honorable man.

—Well, I followed her all afternoon and I was shocked to see her go into the movies alone. Just think, Luz María's

daughter, our own Luz María, who was with us in the
Daughters of the Good Shepherd! But you will say that
the mother is one thing and the daughter is another, reared
in a different epoch. Ay, if only that movie-house could
be closed! I don't mean that the girl really does anything
wrong herself, but the immorality and the kissing in that
picture! I've advised Father Lanzagorta, for the rating is
C 1, to see if she confesses it. I can't tell you how I suffered
watching such kissing, but I hardened my heart and sat
it out. Then I followed her home and heaven knows how
many men flirted with her. I couldn't hear much, for I was
too far behind, but she let herself be stared at by everything
that wore pants. I want you to know about her because right
now Jaime is at a very dangerous age.

—No, sir, my income from taxes isn't what it used to be.
You, sir, of an old family, know that in the old days there
were men of wealth in every village. Not so today! The Revolution chased them all into Guanajuato or to Mexico City.
Only beggars are left. Not only that, but the Party has its
men everywhere and you have to go halves with them! If it
weren't for the splendid way you have handled my invest-
ments, *Don* Jorge, I would be a ruined man. Tell me, is your
little nephew going to inherit your businesses? No, I don't
mean you're ready to retire yet! But an ounce of foresight is
worth a pound of regret, as they say.

—*Dieu et Mon Droit!* Were that still believed, what a
world of infamy we would escape! Poor Jaime Ceballos! It
is going to be very difficult for him to grow up a gentleman
in these times. When Porfirio Díaz mounted the gangplank
of the *Ipiranga,* all taste and respect for private rights went
with him. Vulgarity and administrative rapine took over!
Decency and order ended forever, *sí, señor!*

But the deep sleep of deep roots is something else. It lives
between the pages of the Book which the boy requested for

his fourteenth birthday. Balcárcel observed that to read the Scriptures directly smells of Protestantism. But Ascunción consulted Father Lanzagorta and he had no objection. The dusty old stable, scene of childhood games, was converted into a reading room now . . . reading repeated until the words engraved themselves on the boy's memory. He read in the late afternoons, in the light from the high skylight, until shadows became dark. Between the lines of the big illustrated Bible with thick blue covers, danced words he had heard often before, in his home, but only now was understanding, and doubts were born. He discovered those previously unknown situations that disturb tranquility and give rise to problems like, but far more difficult than, those of algebra. Nevertheless he enjoyed every hour he read. The world was suspended and far away. The universe was only himself, with his back leaning against the old trunk and the heavy book on his knees, himself and the words: *I am come to cast fire on the earth. And what will I, but that it be kindled? And I have a baptism wherewith I am to be baptized. And how am I straitened until it be accomplished?* Those were the words of Jesus being spoken in the very place where Ezequiel Zuno had sat as the boy was sitting now. Fire on the earth. Does every man bring his own torch? Then really to be a man was not to be like the peaceful two men in his family, but to live like Ezequiel, in flames? *Think ye, that I am come to give peace on earth? I tell you, no: but separation. Henceforth shall houses be divided: the father shall be divided against the son, and the son against the father.* Divided, separated, by that other man, the man outside who came from far away. *If any man will come after me, let him deny himself and take up his cross daily and follow me. For whosoever will save his life shall lose it: for he that shall lose his life for my sake shall save it.* Between the lines of the Bible the miner Ezequiel Zuno came back to munch his food and tell Jaime the story of his struggle. Jaime closed his eyes and heard it all again. He heard Zuno's voice, then the clump of boots on paving stones. Would he ever see him again, join him, give up everything and follow him? Informer, informer: another new word that negated the three words that he read: *Woe to you, scribes and Pharisees, hypocrites; because you tithe mint and anise and cummin and have left the weightier things of the law: justice and mercy and faith.*

Then at six he would be called to Rosary in the big bedroom beside the piano so beautifully inlaid and polished. His aunt and uncle would kneel, sometimes along with *Doña* Presentación and *Señorita* Pascualina, and on Fridays Father Lanzagorta would be present to lead them in prayer. *Doña* Asunción lit the candles. And while the familiar voices repeated the familiar words . . . *full of grace, the Lord is with you . . . . . . but deliver us from evil . . . . . . being mindful that thou must die, and knowing that thou knowest not the time nor the place . . . . . . hold me and carry me to Thy heavenly court . . .* Jaime, kneeling too, always near the stiff curtains where the shadows from the candles trembled, would fight the Rosary singsong with very different words: *Woe to you, scribes and Pharisees, hypocrites, because you shut the kingdom of heaven against men: for you yourselves do not enter in, and those that are going in, you suffer not to enter.* And while the keys of the piano moved, Easter Sunday came back, *Für Elise,* and his Aunt Asunción's voice saying: *she* wasn't like us. And then the *Ora Pro Nobis* would seal the linear lips of Uncle Balcárcel, who inwardly was intoning: "Oh, Father, I give Thee thanks that I am not like other men, rapacious, unjust, adulterous; above all that I am not like that publican." That publican was Jaime's mother. *She* was his mother. They were talking about his mother and about Ezequiel Zuno, the outsiders, the unholy ones, the publicans and sinners, all the unclean world to whom the Ceballos family denied entrance to heaven.

Rosary ended. *Señorita* Pascualina named a couple she had

observed embracing and kissing in a dark alley. Father Lanzagorta pompously expressed his satisfaction that there were still left at least a few families capable of setting a good example. *Señora* Presentación reminded them that tomorrow was a Day of Obligation. The candles were put out, the lights were turned on, and they made their way into the green velvet dining room.

"Boy!" said the priest brusquely. "How long has it been since you confessed?"

"A month, Father."

"I shall expect you tomorrow afternoon."

"Yes, Father."

"How many times?"

"Five . . . six . . . I don't remember."

"With whom."

". . . Alone."

"You have never been with a female?"

"No."

"It is the gravest of sins. The sin that most wounds our Lord Jesus Christ. You should feel ashamed. You should weep with shame because you have offended the purity of the Baby Jesus. Would you dare to tell your aunt and uncle about it? They who believe you to be the purest boy in the world? But do no worse, do no worse. When the temptation comes, say an Our Father, and do no worse. Sin against yourself, if you must, but never defile your body with a public woman. You should be disgusted with yourself. You should be thinking that instead of your sinfulness you could be serving the church, you could consecrate your life to the shepherding of souls. Try to convince yourself of that. If you can't, at least have the strength of will not to sin any more against a sacred commandment. Tear these obscene daydreams out of your mind. I forbid you to think of a naked body. I forbid you to think about a woman. I forbid you to think about the pleasures of your own body. I tell you to root out . . ."

"Father, how can I do it?"

"Pray, pray, and keep your thoughts far from women."

"Yes, I want a woman, Father, I confess that too. I want one all the time."

"As your sin is double, so must be your penitence! Don't come back here until you have sincerely repented. I am going to have to talk with your aunt . . ."

"Father! You can't . . ."

"I save souls by every means I can. I refuse to absolve you. It is as if we have merely been talking together."

Others' lives are the preferred topic of conversation at provincial social gatherings. If the life in question is one upon which the speakers may have an influence, their interest multiplies. If the life to be influenced is that of an adolescent, interest becomes duty. And if the adolescent happens to be of rebellious temperament, duty becomes a sacred obligation, almost a crusade.

There are fourteen ladies. They dedicate their Thursday afternoons to embroidering napkins, pillow slips and table-cloths which are then given to a priest. Their meeting place varies from week to week. All of them, for reasons of expediency, maintain social contact with the wives of the rich men of the Revolution. They reserve only these Thursday afternoons for their old-time intimacy. They belong to families who have been friends for generations. The most recent lineage dates from the epoch of Porfirio Díaz. The most ancient reaches far back into colonial times.

"They say that in Mexico City servants are out of the question now."

"My sister-in-law pays her cook two hundred pesos a month."

"No, it isn't possible!"

"You remember the Régules boy, the son of the merchant? Well, when I was in the capital last Christmas I called on him, and his wife told me that she spends three thousand pesos for very ordinary servants."

"Three thousand a year?"

"A month, my dear, a month!"

"Shhhh! For heaven's sake don't let the girl hear! Thank goodness they are still docile enough here. They say that in the capital . . ."

"And yet our sons want to go there to make their fortunes. I've always said that there is nowhere more comfortable than Guanajuato. It's so much nicer to live where everyone knows you and you have real friends."

They embroider, sitting in a circle. Though the drawing room in which they meet changes every Thursday, its elements are always the same: a long narrow room, a barred balcony, high-backed chairs with crocheted doilies, high tables with marble tops, bronze statuary: Winged Victories, barefoot Spanish milkmaids, Dante and Beatrice. An elaborate chandelier. Servants with aprons and braided hair.

"What plans have you made for your nephew, Asunción?"

"Why, he hasn't finished secondary school yet."

"How old is he?"

"Just turned fifteen."

"I saw him on the street the other day. He's a handsome boy."

"Yes, he is, God be praised."

"But what peculiar friends you choose for him."

"Friends?"

"The little Indian boy. They were walking arm in arm."

"I swear that this is the first I know about it, Pascualina. It must be one of his schoolmates."

"Well, *my* boys have gotten tired of inviting Jaime home, for he has never once deigned to say yes . . ."

"He's quite wrapped up in himself, isn't he?"

"Remember how he behaved at that girls' party?"

"It's a wonder he goes anywhere at all. All Guanajuato talks about it."

"Asunción, you don't know how he irritates people. He talks about strange books he has read, and he puts his nose up in the air and acts as if everyone were foolish and frivolous."

"Yes, that's quite true, everyone says that he isn't at all sociable."

"He'll grow out of it, God willing."

"Does he meet his religious obligations?"

"Oh, yes, you know my husband is very strict about that."

"Who do you send him to confess to?"

"To Father Lanzagorta. He wants to go to Father Obregón, who confesses most of his schoolmates."

"I asked because my niece Refugio's son came home from school the other day with a shocking story. He told her that Jaime had stood up right in the middle of class and said that all Catholics are . . . Well, it's really frightful, I'm ashamed to repeat it."

"Go on, woman, go on."

"Asunción is responsible for the boy. She has a right to know."

"Well . . . he said that all Catholics are . . . *hypocrites!*"

"Oh!"

"Mercy! Where did he get such ideas, Presentación."

"Just what I was telling you. The wrong companions."

"And dangerous books."

"My dear, why don't you have him join the Catholic Action? I've had sons that age myself, and I know what it can do for them."

"Yes, adolescent boys must have spiritual guidance."

"First they mix with the wrong sort on the streets. Then they read prohibited books, the next thing they are running around with women, and the end of it is that they become radicals."

"How true! Luisa Ortega's son is a full-fledged communist now."

"Oh, no!"

"Oh, yes. And all because they sent him to school in Mexico City when he was only eighteen! Now they know their mistake, all right."

"Remember how carefully our brothers were reared, Asunción."

"Yes. You're right."

"Although frankly, *your* brother is no shining example. Pardon my bluntness, but . . ."

"Dear God, Pascualina, don't I know it? He has been my cross."

". . . but how *could* he marry that woman?"

"From silk purses to a sow's ear."

"But Jaime has never met his mother. We've reared him ourselves."

"Ay, bad blood will come through, Asunción."

"Librada! Turn on the lights. Shall we take our refreshments now?"

The sun descends. The fingers of the ladies work precisely, expertly. All of them affect clothing a little out of style. Their faces are waxen pale. They sit with their knees tightly pressed together.

What secret and contradictory emotions Asunción feels as Father Lanzagorta, with many euphemisms and many pompous remarks about sacred duties, reveals his conversation with Jaime. When at last the priest leaves, she repeats the old phrase over and over: "Let him always be small! May my baby never grow up!" She realizes suddenly, with an intense but somehow shamed happiness, that the words are foolish now, more foolish than they always were. She looks in the mirror to see if her strange feeling shows, as if looking into the boy's face for the proof of his manhood. Jaime's steps pass in the hall. Her love for him suddenly swells. She goes to a balcony and parts the curtains and sees the boy and Rodolfo come out of the house and walk away. She is pale, a moon behind dark veils. She will not say anything to her husband. She will not repeat what the priest has told her. She will not mention the walks—infrequent now—that the boy takes with his father. She will not speak of the poor peasant boy, Juan Manuel Lorenzo, who has become Jaime's best friend. She will not reveal the secret of the books the boy smuggles into the house like contraband. She feels herself, as never before in her life, a woman: she will let matters move to their natural conclusions, she doesn't want to look ahead, she doesn't want to think about consequences. She watches father and son disappear.

"What does Uncle Balcárcel really do, father?" the boy is saying.

"Do? Why, he works, of course."

"José Mateos, a boy at school, says that uncle steals money from his oldest brother."

"That's not true. How can it be? Your uncle is rich, he doesn't . . ."

"José says that he lends money and then collects it twice over."

"I don't know. I mind my own business."

"Papá, tell me something. Who betrayed Ezequiel?"

"Ezequiel? Who is Ezequiel?"

"The miner who hid in the stable. Don't pretend you don't know about him."

"The fugitive? Oh. But I really don't know. The police came. I was at the store. Your aunt told me."

They walk on side by side. The obese father, every day wearier, with his felt hat pulled down to his ears. The thin nervous youth who does not know what to do with his hands and feet. He buttons and unbuttons the collar of his white shirt.

"It's been so long since we've walked together the way we used to," says Rodolfo. "Do you remember? Let's go to the Fort. I'll tell you the story of Pípila again. You used to enjoy it so."

"Now I'm interested in other stories. In true stories."

"Let it be, let it be," Rodolfo says irritably. "I told you that I don't know. The police came and got him, that's all. Your uncle is a very hard-working and honorable man, and thanks to him . . ."

"And the true story of my mother? Why did you abandon her? Where is she now? I want to meet her!"

For a moment terror paralyzes Rodolfo Ceballos. A moment later he has turned and is fleeing down the street, back toward the house, with his face as gray as a bran cracker. Jaime watches him coldly. The fat clothier is saying over and over: "Nothing has happened, nothing." He himself does not know whether he is talking about a moment ago, his son's terrible question, or the events of sixteen years ago . . .

Warm slow afternoon. Many warm slow afternoons. The new books Juan Manuel Lorenzo lends him. His favorite Book. And now Goya's engravings, and *David Copperfield*, and *Crime and Punishment*. His hateful schoolmates. José Mateos, vaselined hair and face full of pimples, catches Jaime's arm and proposes: "Let's go play with our pricks in front of the girls as they come out of school." Hours of loneliness. He thrusts his hands deep in his pockets and walks in the Jardín del Unión beneath trees clustered with singing birds. He gets lost in unfamiliar neighborhoods of narrow and crooked alleys. He fights against the leaden weight that hangs in his gullet. He fights against his rancor, his hatred, his rebelliousness, against all that is provincial in his life, against the priest Lanzagorta, against the man who betrayed Ezequiel Zuno, against *Señorita* Pascualina, against his father, against himself. His spirit chuckles with the humor of Mr. Micawber, takes on the shadowy flesh of Raskolnikov in a Moscow garret, prostrates itself upon Gethsemani, dances in a Goya aquatint. His heart beats wild because he believes that he can be anything, that the puzzle of the future must work itself out gloriously, that his youth is only a prelude to greatness.

Then abruptly he touches his arms, his flesh, and he feels that it is already too late, that he has already irremediably stained and dirtied the shining body—his own—that first came alive Holy Week. Now he drags himself along like a broken trophy that only a moment before was a triumph. He has promised to go confess to Father Obregón this afternoon. He decides, bitterly, that he will not do it. He will never confess again. He will go directly to Christ. Tomorrow he will take communion with his aunt, but he will not confess. He will not judge, in order to avoid being judged. He will not condemn, in order to avoid being condemned. He will go walking to the Fort with his father again.

So a year passes.

Chapter 6

W<small>HAT IS A YEAR?</small> Mexico's four seasons, almost indistinguishable, which almost may not be felt passing. Summer rain. In fall the smell of smoke. Dry sun-bright winter. Spring's scraping clouds. To sit in a park or the patio at home during vacation months. To watch days go by while an adventure book turns its pages between your hands. Back to school. Learn to get along with your new teachers. Once again to discover your companions changed by the vacation separation:

"I went to the ranch."

"Didn't you know I went to Mexico City? And my cousin took me to a house . . ."

"I learned to ride."

"Aw, I'm fed up with school. Next year I'm dropping out and going to work with my old man."

"Have you ever fucked a girl, Ceballos?"

A year is to turn down pimply Pepe Mateos' invitations to drink a beer or go to a bordel. A year is a Rosary of acts of constriction in your bedroom. A year is the saying over and over in solitude of the greatest Christian words.

April night. The walls of the house are still warm from the

sun. Into every bedroom comes the sound of the great clock in the drawing room. One, two, three, four, all the way to twelve deep-toned gongs; and each who hears mentally visualizes the dance of white wigs and crinolines of the twelve tiny porcelain figures which, when the clock strikes, emerge from the little laquered doors and dance. It is the same clock brought from Madrid by *Don* Higinio. In a moment, Guanajuato's bells will ring midnight too, for ever since *Don* Higinio's era, the clock in the drawing room has always been three minutes fast.

Jaime Ceballos thinks of the sundial in a corner of the damp patio. It marks a different time, and now moonlight shines upon it. His bedroom, like that of his aunt and uncle, opens upon the patio. He squeezes against the plaster wall. He has left his door open, and he smells the saturated night. A green odor of growing plants rises from the patio. From farther away, but stronger, comes the perfume of fields and forests. He thinks again of the sun-numeraled sundial, and sees it as keeping two times: sun hours that are remembered, moon hours that are lost and that he would like to recover.

Night's velvet music reaches the big bedroom where Asunción and Jorge sleep. It is softened by the thick curtains, by the silk sofa, the piano, the high canopy and the mosquito netting of the cedar bed. Night sighs its flutes in Asunción's ears. She opens her eyes and feels beside her the heavy sleeping body of her husband.

The floor of Rodolfo's room on the roof is of volcanic stone. Night belongs to the ants that file between the legs of the iron bed. Rodolfo knows that they are there and he imagines that he can hear them. He yawns and covers his shoulders with the blanket. Yesterday was hot, evening cooled and freshened the air, now night has become warm again, announcing the coming of dawn.

A mosquito buzzes near Jaime's ear. He slaps at it and rolls over against the wall again. The bed was placed against the wall years ago when he was little, so that he would not fall off, and he used to sleep ringed by chairs and cushions. Now he doesn't need them: he is sixteen. Night's insect song invades his head with sensuality bathed in the scents of fruit and damp earth and warm wind.

In the bedroom on the roof, Rodolfo frees his arms from the sheets and crosses them on his chest. He would like to change his sweaty undershirt, but he is lazy and afraid of catching cold. He cannot sleep. He believes it is because he smells beside him the perfume, more tenacious than forgetfulness, of his wife. He raises his fingers to his nostrils, then to his eyes, and tells himself that he is mistaken. He feels beside his body: there is no one. He cups his hands as if to receive flowing water. Her scent has been with him continuously since the afternoon his son spoke of her, and made his skin remember her.

The master bedroom. A yellow moth flutters and Asunción wakes with her mouth open and her hands pressed to her almost virginal nipples. Very cautiously, for she does not want to make any noise, she opens the mosquito netting and tiptoes to the full-length mirror. There she observes herself in the moonlight, drowsy but erect, with her hair falling to her waist and her cheeks flushed by her hot dreams. She tells herself that she is still young and pretty. She unbuttons her gown and displays the round firm breasts which have hardly been touched by a man. No baby has ever sucked there. She does not know why she crosses her arms inside the gown and swells out her stomach and squeezes it. She turns her back on the mirror and looks at the sleeping body of Jorge Balcárcel. No one hears her soft moan. No one sees the hopeless caresses she gives her breasts and belly. She remembers the boy sleeping in the next room. Suddenly she burns with desire to run and see him.

Gray dawn rises from the stones of the patio. The boy, wet from maturbation, forces his chin down into the mattress and with all his strength closes his painful eyes, squeezes his fists, and repeats again and again: *And lead me not into temptation.* Shame and guilt rise up through him from the soles of his feet. He feels that his body is black sand. He sits, then kneels and spreads his arms cross-like. But the words will not come now, and after a moment his dramatic posture seems ridiculous. He gets up and drags the bed away from the wall out into the middle of the room.

The noise of Jaime's bed moving awakens Uncle Balcárcel with a grunt. The mosquito net lies across his face; he removes it and opens his eyes and looks at sleeping Asunción. What the devil racket is his nephew making at this hour of the morning? He sighs and rubs his unshaven face. He thinks about Jaime's future. Various people have warned him about the peasant schoolmate who has become Jaime's inseparable companion. Boys must be protected against their inexperience, Balcárcel tells himself. Life nowadays is full of dangers. He looks for the copper cuspidor beside the bed to spit out the thick morning phlegm. The boy must be specially safeguarded because he is necessary for tranquility in the home; he is everything that he himself—Balcárcel— had not been able to give Asunción. Now he rubs his hair and feels the roughness of his tongue against the roof of his mouth. Yes: the son who because he is not really theirs must be watched over and chained to them more forcefully than if he had sprung from Asunción's barren womb.

But when Balcárcel lets his head fall back against the pillow and disposes himself to sleep placidly again, he does not deceive himself, he freely confesses that the idea of an adolescent, a boy coming to be a man, fills him with disgust. A new sexuality. He cannot support that thought, nor the idea of young love. He is caught suddenly, this most upright man of business, with a series of indecent visions which he wishes and does not wish to disrupt. Then Asunción moves on the bed beside him, opens her eyes and closes her mouth.

"Are you awake?" she says presently.

"It's almost six," her husband responds, rubbing his palm over his stubbled chin.

The woman sits on the edge of the bed and feels her feet into her red slippers. Blue light begins to sift across the room. She covers herself with a shawl and smells the stuffy odors of the night. She goes out onto the corridor that circles the patio, and descends the stone stairs, breathing in the morning. She raps on the windows of the servants' rooms. Her hands rise and she hastily buttons her gown to the throat.

Aunt and nephew have returned from morning Mass at San Roque. The first half of the pews were almost empty, occupied by five or six of the city's gentry. The pews behind were crowded: old women wrapped in black shawls, blue-clad peasants with dark eyes and crossed arms and bare feet smeared with burned clay. *Doña* Asunción counted her rosary as if the beads were pearls; the old women in the rear pews counted theirs as if weighing grains of corn, as if these prayers were the richest part of their overwhelming poverty.

Now the family are gathered in the shadowy dining room beneath the green lamp. A servant has placed, in the middle of the velvet cloth, a fountain of papayas, lemons, cold bananas and sweet-smelling quinces. Jaime holds a quince near his nose. Uncle Balcárcel arches his eyebrows and compresses his thin lips and squeezes lemon juice over a rose slice of papaya. Rodolfo, napkin tucked into his collar, has just covered his mouth with his hand to spit out seeds. Asunción gestures to Jaime that he should wipe something from his right eye. There are smells of fried sausage and bacon.

"Put down that quince and eat," Uncle Balcárcel growls. "I observe that this boy is decidedly skinny."

"He's growing so fast," the aunt says.

"He ought to exercise. What do you do, sir, in your free time?"

"I read a lot, uncle."

"Don't talk with your mouth full." Balcárcel's posture at the table is erect and dignified, as if to contrast with Rodolfo's slumped indolence. The closed fist of his left hand reposes on the tablecloth and now and then he takes his watch from his vest and arches his brows. "Rodolfo, I have no wish to encroach upon your authority. Nevertheless, I am of the opinion that the time has come to speak plainly to Jaime. He is no longer a child, but a young man of sixteen."

The fat merchant becomes all attention. He stops eating.

To speak plainly, Jaime thinks. That is exactly what he wants, to be able to speak and understand plainly.

"Life nowadays," intones Balcárcel, "is replete with dangers. In our youth, Rodolfo, the social atmosphere helped us toward virtue. But today, I am informed, instead of learning discipline, our young people run as free as goats. Nowadays it is held that discipline is wrong, that it is better to give in to one's instincts. No, sir! I say no, sir! Instincts are for brute animals. Men must learn control."

Balcárcel passes his rigid triumphant gaze around the table. Jaime lowers his head.

"I see that my words affect you strongly, young man," the uncle smiles. "All the better. Pray tell me, what is the book you are now reading?"

"A novel, sir."

"A novel. Very good. And what is its title?"

"The Red and the Black."

"Asunción, will you be so kind as to confirm with Father Lanzagorta that this so-called novel is on the Index? You will then have Jaime hand his copy over to you. Let us proceed. Who is your closest friend?"

"A friend from . . . from school."

"His name?"

"Juan Manuel."

"Juan Manuel what?"

"Juan Manuel Lorenzo."

"Asunción, do you call to mind any of our friends whose family name is Lorenzo? Neither do I, neither do I. And I shall tell you why: because these Lorenzos are peasants whose son studies here thanks to a scholarship provided by the government."

"Child, you must be more careful in your associations," says *Doña* Asunción, resting her hand on Jaime's shoulder. The boy is red faced. He looks for words with which to reply to his uncle. He implores the protective intervention of his father. But Rodolfo sits with his hands on his lap and an expression of respectful attention.

"I have not yet concluded," the uncle pronounces with a stiff finger. "And now I enter, decidedly, into the area of your responsibility, Rodolfo. Does it seem to you fitting that a youth whose character is just forming should be led among the lowest classes in the city to attend all manner of rowdy fiestas? At the beginning, I tolerated it, for then Jaime was a child. But now that he is sixteen, I find it decidedly unwise. And the fact is not only that you go with him but that you lead him, Rodolfo, exposing him to loose women and every sort of temptation. You have never felt it fit to tell us about these excursions. There must be a very good reason for that. You will pardon my brutality, but have you by some chance also conducted your son to a house of prostitution?"

The aunt's exclamation is cut short by Balcárcel's rhetorical hand. "Frankness is necessary," he proceeds relentlessly. "Every family must have a head, and I am going to make my authority felt in this one. My first rule shall be that Jaime, like all the young men of our family, must reach marriage pure and chaste and must not know any woman other than the wife God blesses him with. To this end he shall henceforth abandon completely his licentious readings, his degrading friendships, and in one word, his frivolity."

While Balcárcel speaks, dark shame buries itself deep in

Jaime's breast. He is also furious because his father remains mute. The defense that the boy waits for should not be merely a protest, but an active and cutting attack, and should begin with the simple statement: "He is *my* son." His father says nothing, but merely drops his eyes. Finally Jaime summons up all his strength and says quietly:

"Is that how you speak plainly, uncle? With lies?"

Balcárcel flings his arm out. "Leave this table! To your room, sir! To your room without breakfast, to see if fasting will cure you of your insolence! Though your father may be incapable of disciplining you, I shall still show you that in this house there is authority and there will be respect for one's elders!"

The uncle wipes his fingers with his napkin. Jaime rises, begging his father and his aunt for help. They both look down. The boy walks out, to the narrow white room where the servant has already pushed his bed back against the wall.

Smells of abundant provincial breakfast. They eat eggs and sausage in silence. Finally Asunción tries to smile:

"Our cousins are trying to steal the cook. I want you to speak with them, for without Felisa I can't get along."

Balcárcel nods. For the last time he consults his watch, and rises and leaves the dining room. The brother and sister go on eating.

"Tomorrow is the anniversary of Papá's death," Rodolfo says presently.

"Yes. The *Te Deum* will be at ten. Father Lanzagorta."

"What your husband said . . . that Jaime and I, that . . ."

"I know."

"We used to have such good times together. Now we never have anything to say to each other. We just walk, that's all. We don't talk."

"Yes."

"Ever since . . . Asunción, how did he find out? He asked me about Adelina. He told me that I abandoned her."

"You promised never to mention her, never!"

"I didn't mention her. I don't know how he knew. But it's your fault. Yes. Why *did* I abandon her? Because of you."

Birds carol outside, building new nests in the thick spring foliage of the ash trees. Old women creep out of the church of San Roque. Vendors of fruits and candies sing their wares. A cock silently struts along the wall, lording it over his meek hens. His crest is as high and stiff as a bullfighter's flying cloak.

"And now I miss the boy so much, Asunción. He is all I have."

In his bedroom, Jaime feeds and caresses silence. He mutters the mute words of wounded adolescence. He thinks of rebellion, of running away.

Breakfast has ended. *Don* Jorge Balcárcel is now seated in his leather chair in his office, affirming his power over the weak and his servility toward the mighty. Rodolfo Ceballos has now opened the store across the street from the church of San Diego and is unrolling a bolt of cloth. And Asunción is standing outside Jaime's door. Her knuckles lightly rap the glass pane. She raps again and enters. Her face is white and anxious, her hair is up in a knot, her dress is black. She has come to have Jaime love her. She has come to ask him to offer up to her, and to no one else, his solitary youth. And the boy knows it. He remains seated on his bed. Asunción touches his hand.

"Don't be sad, dearest. Your uncle was a little severe. But he thinks only of your own good." The boy does not know how to reply. She continues softly: "We want you to be an upright clean gentleman, like all your ancestors. For you are almost a man now, did you know that? And men . . . are exposed to many dangers. Your uncle and I want to protect you with our experience."

She sighs and crosses her hands.

"Very soon now you are going to . . . to feel desires . . . to

know women. I beg you to have patience and to wait until
you can marry and have a Christian home of your own. Six
or seven years isn't so long, is it? Your uncle and I will help
you to find a good girl. Think about the mistake your own
father made . . ."

"What mistake?" asks the boy, with sudden pain.

"Dearest, your mother was not a woman of our class."

"And of what class am I?" Jaime's face shows disgust.

His aunt straightens herself. She is suddenly the daughter
of proud Guillermina. "You are a Ceballos! Ceballos men
have always been paradigms of gentility!"

She has faced him now and she sees pained mockery in
his eyes.

"A good woman," she goes on slowly, "is harder to find
than a needle in a haystack. Because she is rare, you must
be faithful to her. Your uncle and I will help you choose when
the time comes. Until then, keep your purity as a treasure
for the mother of your sons. Other women . . ." She grows
pale and hesitates. "Other women can infect you with incur-
able diseases, or they will want only your money, like
your . . ."

She stops again, agitated, and swiftly embraces the boy.
"No, I didn't mean to say that. Try to understand me, it is
for your own good." Her voice is indistinct as she caresses
his hands. "We want you to avoid the pitfalls of youth. You're
very good, you know. And other people aren't good at all,
so you need to be careful. You'll always have me to advise
you! No one will ever love you like your mamá Asunción."

And Jaime, caressed by her hands, says for the first time in
his life, without even thinking about it, "Yes, aunt . . ." Aunt
instead of mamá. He feels her tremble: she has received the
word with both pain and happiness. And in the purity of
his untouched love he suddenly sees that she loves him not
as a mother loves a son but as a woman loves a man. The
intuition is unexpected and he could never put it into words.

But he knows that she suspects that he understands now, that he has told her by the way he has drawn smoothly away from her and gone to the flowery wash-basin to dash water across his face. He is surprised and confused. Yet at the same time he feels a little compassion toward a woman who must ask, in this way, a little of love which no man has ever given her.

Asunción suspects, yes, but immediately rejects suspicion. She touches her creamy cheeks and her dark eyelids. Nothing must hint her secret desires; they must remain so secret that she does not know them herself, covered, in the silence of dreams, by vague imagination and over that a black hood of suppression; buried deep in her belly, in the most silent and unknown declivity of her flesh. The voice of truth retreats abruptly into the background of unconsciousness, and her lips speak automatically as she takes out her handkerchief and touches her nostrils:

"Your uncle is quite right. You must not go around any more with that Lorenzo boy. People notice and talk about it. It isn't natural for boys of such different classes to be friends. Promise me that you will not see him again."

Juan Manuel Lorenzo was a pure-blood Indian of small stature and cautious movements. His clear dark eyes looked out at the world with a certain air of surprise, as if he were seeing everything for the first time. It seemed that those eyes understood not by thought, but wholly by intuition.

Four years ago the local government had searched the rural schools for a bright young boy to be given a scholarship for secondary and preparatory studies in Guanajuato city. Juan Manuel had been chosen, and had abandoned his childhood world of goats and adobe huts to move to the state capital. He lived in a boardinghouse, in a little six-by-nine cubbyhole of a room, and in the afternoons and evenings supported himself by working in the railroad shops in Irapuato. His tiny room was hardly large enough for the piles of books he had there. Every month he bought a volume of a Spanish classic and devoured it in two nights, reading in the light of the single bulb hanging from the ceiling. His Spanish possessed a certain cautious quality: it was a learned language, learned with deliberation. Like his slow physical movements, his speech made him appear—at school, at work, in the rooming-house—as neither dull nor brilliant, but merely different. He evoked a sense of strangeness. His private tenacity and concentration were converted publicly into a certain rudeness that was wholly inoffensive, an essential and vigorous simplicity which the soft manners of an Indian peasant boy transplanted to the city were not enough to conceal. If his body was tiny, his head was enormous, and jar after jar of gummy goo were not enough to dominate his stiff hair, which bristled like a prickly pear. In spite of this, no one could call Juan Manuel ugly. Those dark eyes, wide open to the world and iluminated by an inner happiness, were lights in a face full of energy and strength of will. His simple gestures possessed a real elegance. His defenseless naturalness inspired respect, and saved him from the treatment which the boys of his school reserved for one of his low station in life.

Juan Manuel thought of Guanajuato as a room no larger than its occupant, as a paradise closed to many, magic in its stone labyrinths and its changing colors. Every Saturday afternoon he and Jaime Ceballos would walk together through the winding alleys and across the little plazas. The city itself was the academy for their wakening intellects. And what, indeed, is the first and truest school of personal discovery? Long slow strolls, almost wordless, with a trusted friend our own age, the first who treats us as a man, the first who listens to us, who shares a passage from a book with us, a germinating idea, a new dream. That was what Juan Manuel and Jaime gave each other on their Saturday walks. A city of open windows was stimulus to their curiosity. In the narrowness of the rising and falling, twisting old 17th-Century streets, a honeycomb of life was exposed. Behind this barred window sits a yellow skinned old woman counting her rosary into the air; behind that one, five bibbed children grip the bars and sing childhood songs; in the next, a blushing girl lowers her eyes and reaches her hand through to her sweetheart on the street. Beds are made, socks are darned, the pleasant air is taken, gossip is exchanged and commented upon, eyes stare at what passes, someone waits in a rocker for death to come, new life gestates to the rhythm of knitting, floors are swept and vigil is held over the dead, and all before open windows, in clear view; but at the same time strangely silent, strangely still. A dark solitude oppresses this so-open life. What in another latitude, among different people, would be fiesta and riotous communication, in Guanajuato is mute, tense, life's silent flow between the cradle and the grave.

Now Juan Manuel, dressed in tan cotton pants, a white shirt, and yellow shoes, was standing in the alley beside the Ceballos mansion with his eyes raised to the stable skylight. He had just whistled to signal Jaime that he was waiting. Against his side he held a notebook and several books. He lent Jaime books often; the last was Stendhal's novel. It was more difficult for the rich boy to buy books than for the poor one, for Juan Manuel possessed an independence that was completely lacking in Jaime. The Balcárcels, moreover, exercised strict censorship, and Jaime had to smuggle in the books—always an annotated volume, underlined, of the cheapest edition, quick to lose its cardboard covers.

Jaime appeared at length and the two friends greeted each other and walked off across the plaza, Jaime's hand on Juan Manuel's shoulder.

"Have you read . . . *The Red and the Black* yet?" Juan Manuel asked presently.

"They took it away from me. They say it's prohibited."

They took a well-known route, the Callejón de los Can-taritos. Juan Manuel walked in silence, with his face sad. Jaime, though he had the impulse, did not dare to offer to buy a new copy of the lost book.

"Your aunt and uncle, Ceballos . . ." Juan Manuel hesitated, as he did habitually; his speech was all starts and stops, though it was also precise. "Do they understand the book so clearly?"

To use surnames was one of their tacit conventions. It was one of their ways—a little eccentric, perhaps a little ridiculous —of showing their mutual respect. To Ceballos in the begin-ning it had been hard to call Lorenzo by a name that so little resembled a surname. Nevertheless, Juan Manuel did not pronounce "Lorenzo" as if it were a given name; he prolonged and accented the second syllable, letting the last syllable die almost soundlessly: "Lo-*rennn*-zo." Jaime learned to pronounce it that way too, and the young Indian showed his pleasure by his shining eyes.

"What part of the book . . . most impressed you?"

"You know, Lorenzo . . ." Jaime crossed his arms on his chest and frowned. "There is one place where he says that all great actions should be extremist when a great man does them. And then he points out that it is only when it is all over that the action appears great to ordinary people."

"By extremist you mean a . . . a radical action."

The friends also showed their respect for each other by their very careful way of expressing their ideas. Jaime wrinkled his nose. "It seems a sound rule to me. That is how Christians should act. It is how Christ acted. And they treated him as a crazy man, a radical, as you say, and today everyone is his disciple. Disciples of a maniac."

"I fear," said Lorenzo with his habitual pause, "that faith based upon the example of one single individual, by repeti-tion must become caricature. Christianity has been carica-

tured . . . by the clergy, by aristocracies, by rich people . . .
Am I explicit?"

"If it were only caricature!" Jaime smiled. "It is even less,
Lorenzo. I always think of caricature as somehow rebellious.
Your Goya drawings, for example. My aunt Asunción found
them in my room and yelled to high heaven. She said how
could I have those indecent and horrifying apes that made
her skin crawl. Wasn't that just what Goya wanted . . . that
people like my aunt should feel offended and shocked?"

"Sometimes it is the only weapon against . . . an unjust and
hostile world."

Now, at the intersection with Los Positos, the long narrow
street of dull yellow and blue became level, and the air was
sweet with the scent of many bakeries.

"Smell!" said Lorenzo.

"So for you the most valuable action is not an individual
one?"

"The most valuable? Isolated . . . no. What is important
is to be part of a general action, a movement. I want to tell
you something, Ceballos . . ."

Jaime walked ahead and bought two sugar-covered cream
puffs. He gave one to Juan Manuel, who bit into it with great
delicacy. A mustache of sugar dust formed on his upper lip.
He went on:

"The government gave my father a little plot of land . . .
to farm. That was good, very good. It was generous. Just
the same, the plot is very small . . . large enough for a few
cabbages and turnip greens, and that's all. Corn won't grow
there. . . . So my father has to look for work again. He gets
into debt again with a *patrón*. But all we eat is cabbage and
turnip greens. Our condition . . . really isn't changed, it is
really just what it was before. My father can't do anything
about it . . . alone. Everyone must unite. Before . . . centuries
ago . . . the land belonged to everyone. Every farmer had
his share . . . and moreover had a share in what everyone

produced. Now, instead of that, everyone has his own plot today . . . but none of the plots is large enough, and there is no sharing. Because we are so poor . . . and unlucky . . . no one can accomplish anything. But all together . . . that's what they have to understand . . . all together."

When Juan Manuel spoke like this, Jaime was always surprised. To him Lorenzo was not a peasant but an intellectual boy fed and consumed in a fever of study. Juan Manuel's single light bulb burned until dawn; night after night his face grew thin over his books. His big disheveled head between his hands, his elbows resting on his little table, he devoured page after page, took notes, debated with himself, refused to admit a single statement by the invisible author without first putting it in doubt and seeking its reasoning. The cautious difficulty with which he spoke to others was converted, in these interior monologues, into implacable eloquence. Nietzsche, Stendhal, the Andreiev of *Sachka Yegulev*, Dostoievsky, Dickens, Balzac, Max Beer, Michelet, these were his nightly interlocutors, and Calderón, Tirso, Berceo. But although the boy could lose himself in intellectual labor, he could never forget his humble origin and the problems of his people. Precisely to the degree that his thought deepened during those long warm or cold hours in his tiny room, in the Mediterranean of his sixteen years, he resolved with greater ardor to unite the lessons of his reading with the conditions of the life he had known. He began in those days to investigate the whole literature of the Mexican Revolution.

Jaime Ceballos read and labored less than his friend, but dreamed more, and grasped deeper the two or three ideas which he believed important. Like Lorenzo, like any adolescent, he felt safer talking to himself with closed eyes than he would have speaking to those persons he would really have liked to address, his father and uncle and aunt. In solitude he could tell them what he thought; facing them, he could not overcome his uncle's cold air of authority, his aunt's sentimental lack of comprehension, his father's simple weak confusion. How could he possibly have suggested to humble timorous Rodolfo that he ought to have the manhood and the rectitude to assume his responsibility toward Adelina? How could he have informed his pious aunt that the sin is not to be a woman but to be hypocritically a woman? How could he, finally, have asserted that he himslf, Jaime Ceballos, was a living person, and thus oblige his uncle to respect him as he was and for what he was? How could he have made clear to Balcárcel that it is more important to love virtue than to fear vice? And how could he have pointed out to all three of them that insofar as they called themselves Catholics, they ought to behave as Christians; that they should either really practice Christianity or give up naming themselves followers of a faith to which they gave only lip-service? No, when Uncle Balcárcel's finger raised and his thin lips moved, Jaime's own voice was paralyzed. And this lack of response to his never asked questions had given the boy conviction that he could alone, without communication with anyone, prove that everything he asked of others was really possible.

Not even to Juan Manuel did he fully disclose this decision, hugged close and repeated in the solitude of his adolescence as the only treasure of a dawning manhood continuously attacked by his own doubts and self-pity and by the doubts and self-pity of the three adults close to him.

"Diego Rivera, magnificent painter, was born in this house December 13, 1886." So read a plaque on the ocre yellow wall of a house on Los Positos. The two boys walked in silence. Jaime put his arm around Juan Manuel's shoulder.

At that moment *Señorita* Pascualina passed stiffly. Her *pince nez* framed eyes opened wide. With a haughty and angry air she adjusted her black bonnet above her yellow face. "A Ceballos!" she hissed at Jaime.

Lorenzo spoke again:

"Do you remember the part where the author says . . . that Julien had a marvelous eloquence? I think he spoke well because . . ."

"Because he didn't have to act like a man of the time of Napoleon," Jaime interrupted. He was angry about his meeting with *Señorita* Pascualina, who would certainly go tell Aunt Asunción, this very afternoon, that he and Juan Manuel had been walking arm-in-arm.

They were silent. Jaime was imagining a world of freedom in which boys his age could run away from home and in a few months of an Egyptian campaign gain the golden insignia of full colonels. Every soldier would have a marshal's baton in his knapsack. Reading about the Napoleonic wars had always excited him: he imagined himself in the middle of the great battles, baptized by the great names which according to the encyclopedia were inscribed upon the Arch of Triumph in Paris. Wagram, Austerlitz, Jena, Smolensk, the Pyramids, Friedland. Uniforms, the stampede of cavalry, Moscow in flames, that strange snowy conflagration. And the mysterious women who trailed history's pages: Josephine, Marie Walewska. And palaces: Fontainebleau, Marly, Versailles, Chantilly. And the tangle of intrigue and adventure behind the names of Fouché and Talleyrand.

"Have you read *War and Peace?*" Jaime said.

"No."

"It's very long. For vacations."

Juan Manuel's thoughts were also wandering slowly and silently. He was transferring the flaming actions of which Stendhal had written to other men upon other battlefields. Villa's cavalry in the Bajío. The Yaqui Indians who had won at Celaya for Obregón. Zapata ambushed in Chinameca. Now all these heroes were dead, and in their place were Julien Sorels, who prattled so eloquently about the Revolution.

"I'm going to lend you a book by Vasconcelos, Ceballos."

Juan Manuel passed his thin hand over his shock of rebellious hair. At times during the long hours he spent reading, he was stopped by a question that puzzled him: why was it that certain men in certain times spoke in one manner and others in other times in a style so different? On the one hand, Vasconcelos' passionate tumult; on the other, the serene clarity of Guzmán. And why had both these men spoken in accents of truth, though in opposing styles, about the same subjects which in other lips were lies? He recalled speeches of farm agents in his village and of the union leaders at Irapuato, and newspaper editorials, and addresses by politicians. This was the other Mexican language: a language of lackeys.

The two young friends walked suspended in thought, far from the quiet traffic of Guanajuato's winding streets. Lampposts came on suddenly and an organ grinder began to crank out a march in front of a window of tiny immobile children who seemed to be staring at the world's theatre for the first time and from the first row.

There ought, Juan Manuel reflected, to be a language which would not only reflect but could also transform reality. He would have liked to explain this to his friend. But he did not have the right words for his intuition.

They descended Juan Manuel's street. The boardinghouse, an old mansion of whitewashed brick, smelled of fried beans. The landlady was in one of the front windows, a spinster who always wore white gloves, and she greeted Juan Manuel and Jaime with her peering head. When the two friends reached the patio, she was waiting there, abject, wrapped in a print shawl, the heels of her laced boots tapping the stones.

"Young man!" her shrill voice cried. "The girl tells me that she can hardly get into your room now. Those books catch so much dust. After you leave, no one will want the room, and I am not disposed, listen to me well, to spend money for nothing."

"I'm sorry, *señora*. It's my work." Juan Manuel walked on toward the stairs.

"Young man! You owe me for the month!"

"I'll be paid at the shop tomorrow, *señora*," said Juan Manuel without turning.

"*Señorita!* How many times do I . . ."

They climbed the narrow worn stairs. Worm-gnawed ceiling beams dripped. Plaster had flaked from the walls, and black butterflies were concealed in the high shadows. At the end of the narrowest hall, Lorenzo opened a door of flowery curtains and they entered the tiny room full of books piled beneath and at the foot of the iron cot.

"Here's Vasconcelos' book. I have to go to the shop now. Today I'm working overtime."

"I'll go with you."

Jaime reflected that by now *Señorita* Pascualina had communicated her gossip to Aunt Asunción, who would be looking for him all over the house to protect him from a quarrel with Balcárcel . . . who would go straight to his—Jaime's—bedroom to make sure that his obedient nephew had not left it all day. But the fear of new punishment was less imperious than the adventure of disobedience.

"Yes, I'm going with you," he repeated, excited by pale descending darkness.

They went out on the street, brothers by a communication without words. They squared their shoulders, breathed deep the thin air, and marched half strutting to the corner where the Irapuato busses passed.

"If there is work tomorrow, I can come," Juan Manuel told the foreman when they finished. He wiped his forehead, smeared his arm with a streak of grease. Jaime stood beside him with his jacket hanging from a hooked finger. Both boys' shirts, like their faces, were spotted with soot and oil. Jaime felt a new happiness. He hugged himself, enjoying the soreness of his muscles.

"You don't have to come," said the shop foreman. He smiled and rumpled Juan Manuel's bristly black hair. "Take the weekend off. Does your friend want to begin next week too? There's plenty of work."

"No," said Juan Manuel.

"Sure I do," said Jaime.

"Good. Juan Manuel can explain to you a little about gears and oils, and if you want to you can work together Monday."

They walked out of the shop onto the big yard, a landscape of steam and machines. From the high cabins of locomotives, engineers greeted Juan Manuel with their caps, as if thanking him because their engines were running well.

"You worked hard, Ceballos. Since they didn't pay you this time, let me invite you to have a beer."

"Did you see that?" Jaime exclaimed when a worker passed and said hello to them and slapped Jaime's shoulder. "Now we're the same!" He spoke with happiness, but immediately he was afraid that he had offended Juan Manuel. But Juan Manuel's smile broadened. They did not speak again until they reached the little building, half a bar and half a grocery, which was hidden beneath a tarpaper roof on the edge of the yard.

"Two *Superiores*," Juan Manuel said to the goat-faced man who was uncapping bottles.

They waited, hot and panting, with their arms on the fly-specked counter. They drank the opaque liquid eargerly. Juan Manuel leaned his head on one hand.

"How are you going to get permission from your aunt and uncle?"

"They can't keep me from working, can they? I'm grown now. Hasn't Uncle always said that I have to be a hard worker?"

The bar began to fill with laborers who arrived thirsty

and stained with grease. Some of them called to Juan Manuel
by name, others raised a hand to their caps and nodded to
both boys. Jaime sniffed the lip of his brimming glass. He
filled his mouth with foam. He would have liked to tell Juan
Manuel that this was the first complete day of his life as a
man. But his sense of pleasure was followed by one of mockery as he thought of his aunt and uncle angry or uneasy or
whatever they might be. The bar was heavy with smoke. A
worker elbowed Juan Manuel. Three women had entered,
harnessed for combat. Two of them were young, the other
old and thin. The young woman leading was short and fat,
and the girl beside her was tall and heavy-legged. Both of
them were thickly made-up, in startling contrast to the third,
who with her long straight hair and her scrubbed face looked
more like a nun than a whore.

"Meche!" cried a voice from the back of the room, and the
girl in front pushed her way toward it. The other two elbowed
places for themselves at the counter. "What will it be, Fina?"
said the tall girl to her yellow-skinned companion.

"Do you have enough for a cognac?"

"It's not eleven yet, drink a beer. Easy to see why they
call you Fina!"

The tall girl lifted her arm and her glass while looking at
Juan Manuel and Jaime. Juan tried to smile, Jaime lowered
his eyes.

"Come on, Fina, drink to the boys."

"They ought to be home in bed," the skinny woman said.
She shook a finger in front of her companion's face. "And
you better remember that tomorrow is Sunday and ask God
to forgive you!"

The tall girl laughed loudly and grabbed the passing arm
of the man behind the counter: "Just listen to Fina, Gomitos.
Always pretending to be so holy."

"I don't pretend, I am." The thin woman held her beer
bottle between both hands.

"I'm glad that we worked together today," said Juan Manuel.

"I had a friend once, Lorenzo. His name was Ezequiel."

"What you don't understand, Gomitos, is that Fina don't let any man touch her. She goes around with us trying to keep us on the straight and narrow." She laughed again.

"I've never told anyone about him, Lorenzo."

"With you and Meche, I'm sure wasting my time," Fina grumbled.

"He was a miner who hid in the stable because the police were after him. He had led a strike at the mines."

"Because you're so silly. Instead of going around preaching, you ought to find some old man you can make happy," tall Lupita answered, with great guffaws.

"Who could have betrayed him, Lorenzo? Ever since, that's what I've thought about. But from today on, thanks to my work with you, I think I'm going to do something for Ezequiel."

"Ingrate! But when something goes wrong, who do you come to, begging to be prayed for? To old Fina, who always listens to your troubles."

"We better be starting back to Guanajuato," Jaime said. But Juan Manuel, smiling, indicated that he still had half a bottle left. A locomotive and cars passing outside drowned their voices.

"The crew for Ciudad Juarez!" someone shouted from the door. Several men in overalls departed, wiping their mouths with their sleeves. The sounds of the yard grew louder or fainter. They were deep-toned noises, a rumble in the earth, and the little bar seemed to tremble.

"This Fina," Lupita said to the man behind the counter, "gives herself airs because she says she was a real society lady in Guanajuato once. Claims she had a rich husband."

"What, didn't he leave you anything?" Gómez of the long face asked with complete seriousness.

"How much?" asked Juan Manuel.

"Lies, all lies," laughed Lupita as she adjusted her brassiere and hummed: ... *I left my spring years in saloons* ...

"One peso."

Fina's yellow face burned red and she pushed it near Lupita's blue lips and in an intense muted voice spat out: "Adelina López lived in the biggest house in Guanajuato, with servants and chandeliers and silver knives, and received all the aristocrats, people that in your whole life you have never even seen!"

"Four pesos change," said Gomitos.

Adelina's words came to Jaime's hearing suffocated by the racket of cars and engines outside. They arrived long after they were pronounced, when Lupita had already replied something and was saying to the man behind the counter:

"Gomitos, what are you going to be doing after work?"

Jaime raised his face and his eyes devoured the profile of transparent bones, the sad defensive eyes, the pale untinted lips, the dark and gray hair of the woman who had said that she was his mother. He stared at his beer bottle and discovered his own face, sweaty, smeared by labor, distorted by the curvature of the glass. He went outside without waiting for Lorenzo. Even there he could hear Adelina's last words:

"I don't do this because I need to. I come to save you, all of you."

As Jaime stepped off across the ties between rails shining in torchlight, he felt the cold night on his damp back, and he tried to pull together the fragments of a body that seemed to have come apart, while Adelina shook her finger under the nose of laughing Lupita and went on:

"I'm bored, that's why I'm here, because I'm so bored."

"Rebel! Obstinate rebel! You shall spend one week in your room on bread and water, and we'll see who lasts longer. My father used to say that discipline begins with a good caning. Decidedly, you are straining my patience. Nevertheless, I shall be generous this time."

But Jaime did not hear his uncle. On his stomach on the bed, with his arms hanging, wearing the same grease-stained shirt and pants, he felt that the lead weight that had hung so long in his throat had finally come loose and was moving boiling through his veins. He could no longer resist his pain, his hatred, his sense of strangeness. He dug his fingers into the bed-springs and sobbed, thinking of Ezequiel Zuno and Adelina López. No, the words of the Bible did not explain faith, but those two names, those two living people who had suffered hurt at the hands of the living people who formed his family. Weekly communion, daily prayers, novenas and Mass and processions: Rodolfo, Asunción, Uncle Balcárcel, all in black with their eyes full of pious self-satisfaction, kneeling in the church with mouths open to receive the Host; and Ezequiel, and Adelina.

But you aren't alone, and that's the problem, that no one is alone.

I don't do this because I need to. I come to save you, all of you.

The walls repeated it. The compact view from his window, when he rose and stood there, repeated it. Steps passing along the alley repeated it. And those words were the only words in the world that meant anything to him.

He fell on the bed again. The servant came with his bread and water and a bit of sugar candy, Asunción's gift, hidden in the napkin. Balcárcel had forbidden his wife and Rodolfo to visit Jaime. Jaime dampened the bread and swallowed it without chewing. He buried his face in the bedspread.

There were hours when his mind was empty, and other hours when words and faces passed at a gallop. Sometimes his eyes burned with wish for a cataclysm which would at one terrible blow annihilate all Guanajuato; a bolt of lightning which would leave the Ceballos mansion in ashes. Coward, Christian, coward, Christian, coward, Christian. And now daylight had made the closed curtains glow again. He woke from his brutal vigil repeating words senselessly. Would he ever really speak? Would he make anyone understand, would he communicate anything? "You are almost grown now," Ezequiel Zuno had said. No one else knew or believed that. To be a man. To leave home, to love a woman, to discover buried treasure. To return and avenge himself. To be a man . . .

The bedroom warms. The boy thinks of death, and decides that the death of those who have not been loved must be sweet and serene; he imagines his mother dead, sweet and serene in repose. Sounds of day begin. The bells of passing mules. Vendors' cries. Distant autos. Words: *Well did Isaiah prophesy of you, hypocrites, as it is written: This people honoreth me with their lips, but their heart is far from me. And in vain do they worship me, teaching doctrines and precepts of man. For leaving the commandments of God, you hold the traditions of men . . .*

The servant enters again and Jaime gives her the smelly chamberpot. He paces the room in his bare feet. He tries to close the curtains completely. Again words whirl: They offend you, Lord, they offend you when they betray a man or abandon a woman; they offend you when they sell or humiliate someone, in order not to be sold and humiliated themselves; they offend you because you promised that your sacrifice would not be in vain. They offend you, Lord. The silent afternoon. The whole city in siesta. He tries to sleep; his growling empty stomach will not let him. When night falls, he opens his curtains and stares out. A persistent hallucination forces him to seek in the dying horizon light for the voice that will have to answer him. *Why doth this generation seek a sign? Amen, I say unto you, a sign shall not be given to this generation.* No, Father: give me a sign that I may know I am not alone. Job waited and saw God.

He urinates and returns to bed.

When he wakes again, he discovers for the first time that he has a beard. Not only the few isolated hairs that he has trimmed with scissors. He stands in front of his mirror. How many times has he observed himself there since he was thirteen? How that glass face has fascinated him! What lay behind the sad eyes? Why did the thin neck tremble? Why did he feel so alone?

"I trust you are benefitting from your lesson," says Uncle Balcárcel, who is lazily observing the boy contemplating himself. Jaime's startled hand picks up the scissors and his arm rises. His uncle remains impassive.

"I have no doubt but that you'll try to kill me. Every passing day reveals more of the perversity of your nature."

Jaime lets the scissors fall.

His thin nervous figure contrasts with the complacent rhomboidal one of his uncle. They look at each other in silence. The air smells of dawn, light enters with full hands, the sun hangs in the middle of the window. Laurels stir in the plaza. Paving stones of the alleys are wet. The droning saw of a cabinet-maker, bells of mules, they cry of the knives-sharpener, steps descending to Mass in San Roque. At his back, Jaime hears the world.

Balcárcel rubs his stomach, his index fingers hooked in the pockets of his vest. "Are you finally going to tell me where you were Saturday night?"

"You know already. That busybody *Señorita* Pascualina told you."

"You can't have spent the night walking with your peasant friend."

"No. I spent it learning who you are, and who my father is . . . My God, my father! How could he . . ."

Balcárcel's eyes do not question. His face will remain im-

mobile, say what the boy may. "I have never found it pleasant to speak of unpleasant subjects, Jaime. Life is difficult
enough for me to insist that in the home we avoid disagreeable conversations. But now that I find you so changed, it is
well that we understand each other. And I am sure that what
I have to say to you is decidedly more important than anything you have to say to me."

Jaime wants to raise his voice, but it sinks to a whisper:
"You betrayed Ezequiel Zuno . . . you let my mother be
thrown out on the street! All you do is talk about morality.
You and everyone in this house, jabber, jabber about religion,
while you do everything that is not religious . . ."

"These recent days I have conversed first with Father Lanzagorta and then with Father Obregón. Decidedly you are
not the one to discuss morality and religion. Do I surprise
you? *Sit down*, you're a bundle of nerves."

The sun strikes the boy's back as he sits on the bed. How
quickly it has risen. Balcárcel paces back and forth in front
of him stroking his belly while his patent leather shoes
squeak.

"I understand your attitude quite well. You are an impure
boy, and because you were afraid to confess your sins, you
stopped going to Father Lanzagorta."

Balcárcel turns and observes his nephew with satisfaction.
He clasps his hands behind his back and lowers his face:
"Father Obregón has told me that you have never confessed
to him, not even once!"

"Why do you worry so much about sin?" the boy's voice
struggles. "Why don't you think sometimes about the good
things in life?" He retreats to the corner of the bed.

"Sins! Good things! Cynic! You have stained Christ's body.
You have taken communion without first confessing! You
are a cowardly and sacrilegious boy! Yes, sacrilegious!"

"And what is it called to betray a man, Uncle?"

"We have nothing further to discuss."

"And to put my mother out on the street, to force her to go around with whores and . . ."

"Shut up, you idiot! I'm losing my patience! It was a mistake for us to take you into this home, to think that we could make anything out of you. Criminals, peasants, whores, these are your great loves!"

"One doesn't choose the people one loves, and I love them and hate you."

Balcárcel's red hand slaps the boy's chin. Jaime defends himself with his legs. Finally, he kicks his uncle in the groin and doubles him over.

All morning, lying in bed, Jaime remembers that moment: his uncle holding his belly, himself trembling, begging forgiveness. He remembers how Balcárcel left the bedroom, mute, threatening with an open palm.

Then it all seems far away. The boy rests. He feels calm. Evening bells ring. A musty odor rises from the alley: the night of sleeping dogs and cold stones has begun to gather there. In the evening silence the figures of Ezequiel Zuno and Adelina López draws near again. The words of people alone and mistreated may be heard again. Jaime's anger is spent. His argument with his uncle blurs in memory and takes on the grotesque unreality of a pantomime. A ray of light opens in his mind. He no longer needs to ask others to do anything. He ought not to blame even his uncle. He must ask of himself alone; himself alone must act and do something for Ezequiel's sake, for Adelina's sake, in the name of Asunción, in the names of Rodolfo and Balcárcel.

He sleeps deep, certain that tomorrow he will write his name across the firmament. He sleeps embracing his pillow. The voice which wakes him is the voice that has persisted, chanting, through his dream: *For I am not come to call the just . . .*

Chapter 7

. . . but sinners . . .

His shoes leave the hardness of the pavement and with surprise stop upon soft earth. The countryside opens before him. A yellow road winds between fields of pale wheat and high corn. The deep narrow valley rises, slowly flattening, until it reaches a stream.

Jaime descends with his feet buried to the ankle in black loam. He waits for a moment beside the stream; beyond it a straw-colored plain undulates in the early wind, stretches all the way to the line of mountains, hazy in dawn. Behind him the morning bells of Guanajuato's churches are ringing. He leaves the path and slips off his shoes and lifts his eyes to a sun rising through shreds of vapor. The air is cool, but the earth is already warm. Guanajuato grows small and toy-like behind him. A hill stands high on the plain. Beyond it the boy can see the plain sweeping on, crossed by dark briary gulleys. He is surrounded by the living earth. Newborn thrushes chirp. Buzzards circle overhead.

Once past the hill his way becomes harder. Brambles and briars catch at his legs, stones bruise the soft soles of his feet, the air cuts his skin, sweat glues his shirt to his back. There is a different vegetation along the sides of the ravine now, gray and brown, spiny, for the lake has not extended its fingers of water this far. This is untilled land, where a few goats tinkle their bells. Then the bald mountain, a castle of rock and briars. The arid stone tumult of the Mexican desert. Stone and dust and flapping black wings. Ravines and cliffs, solitude, the mountain's closed fist. The land original, obstinate, beyond salvation, which refuses to accept man; autonomous nature, a kingdom that will not be divided.

He takes off his shirt. His face is not calm, it reflects his profound anxiety. The palms of his hands are wet. He picks up the broken shell of a wild egg. Was it a bird's womb, or a lizard's? The sun burns his shoulders. His erect body is almost lost in the vast panorama. He stoops and begins to collect long sharp cactus spines, which he laces and plaits into a whip. Air is a hot lung in which the sun can be heard panting.

His hand holds the whip and rises. Ezequiel, bound, is led before him again. Adelina sucks her glass of beer. The whip of thorns and cactus needles lashes down upon his bare back. He bites to hold in the cry of pain. Again the whip falls cuttingly. Thorns stick into the flesh of his back and he must jerk to free the whip. He waits a little before the next blow. A needle-sharp briar digs into his chest just below the nipple; as he pulls it loose, he feels his flesh tear. And the sun looks on, his only witness. He falls on his knees. His eyes cloud as they see his dripping blood. Why has pain made him happy? He was not searching for happiness. Kneeling on the hard earth he raises the whip again and again, and lashes himself without pity. The hot sun mixes with the blood clotting on his back. A cactus spine catches him in the genitals and for the first time he screams.

He falls forward on his face. Air is heavy, motionless over his exhausted body. To breathe in is cold, to breathe out hot. A small curious lizard, dirt-colored, approaches his tired mouth. The boy watches the lizard slowly roll over, and it is as if the earth has rolled over and he is now hanging upside down in empty space. He tightens his eyes and feels the terror of a universe of wandering stars contained within another greater universe which is contained within another still greater, where the vastest worlds are scarcely dust, particles in an endless sidereal ocean. The tiny lizard scurries back under a stone.

Time stops. There is an hour when he feels only his body's heaviness. The sun is burning directly overhead. There is no wind now and the boy's body buries itself against the trembling earth. Tired dust dances beyond his nostrils. The sun licks his wounds with a burning tongue. His stomach shivers.

Then the hour of new wind, when brush begins to sigh again and the cicadas wake from their siestas. The hour of his first spoken prayer, pronounced slowly by a voice that has never stopped praying silently since it first learned words.

A buzzard slowly, avidly descends, ready to pounce. Jaime smells it before he feels the talons on his back. With a guttural gasp he beats away the black wings and he shrieks until the ravine echoes: "Let me be . . . like you . . . not the lie . . ."

The sun hangs over its red lake rimmed by mountains. His words are overpowered by that splendor. But, one with the earth, he would like to speak to the earth, saying: *I did it for them. For all of them and for each of them, because nothing is gained cheaply, because all evil must be punished. Because someone must step forward and accept what others are afraid of.*

He rises painfully and puts on his discarded shirt. The cloth scratches like sharkskin. His legs will hardly support him. Night has awakened with a thousand voices of luminous insects. A vague glow indicates his path. He walks back feeling something good in every stone and brush he stum-

bles against. Suddenly his lips encounter the wispy fingers
of wheat. He has returned. Wheat stubble bends beneath his
bare feet and he hurries toward a path soft with watercress.
A forest of trees tells him that he is near the city again.

There he stops, with his eyes whirling crazily. A sweaty
horse crosses through the shadows and its tail whips his face.
This nearness of a living being draws the first tears of pain;
the slime of consciousness stirs and the waters begin to flow.
He sees men galloping across fields with raised rifles and
copper eyes and singing spurs. Sounds, so strange after the
silence of the long day, begin to come together. A trembling
in his throat and he has reached the city, its high domes, its
towers and its stone and painted walls. Guanajuato of the
honorable merchant *Don* Higinio Ceballos. Guanajuato
where Grandfather Pepe made the family fortune and filled
drawing rooms with French chandeliers. Guanajuato where
Uncle Pánfilo guarded the safe full of gold pesos. Guanajuato
where Papá Rodolfo wasted his youth. Guanajuato, lorded
over by Uncle Balcárcel's green face and sententious tongue.
City of the righteous, of the family of those who have never
done evil. Home of the exalted.

A dark woman carrying a jar on her head passes. The first
pavement stones. Little lights of tanneries and blacksmiths'
shops. The swinging doors of beer-smelling bars. Surprised
brown burros. The plaza. The huge mansion. Jaime's face
squeezes with pain; his wounds, blood mixed with dirt, burn;
he falls on stones that glisten beneath the streetlight, and
his hands claw at the green gate.

"I cannot understand the boy. Decidedly, I cannot understand him." Balcárcel crossed his hands behind his back in
a way that inflated his chest and spread the lapels of his coat.
"What did he tell you?"

In spite of the swift evening air the bedroom held a
closed-in stale smell. The velvet curtains preserved among

their stiff pleats the low voices of the past: this had been the bedroom of the Spanish grandparents who had made love here with tenderness and grace, then that of Pepe and rigid Guillermina, then that of the brief incomprehension between Adelina and Rodolfo. A century of garments had hung in the mahogany wardrobe: bustles, greatcoats, white leggings, Manila cloaks, silk hats, Prince Alberts, bright boas, tuxedos, ostrich feathers, straw hats, canes with incrusted handles, umbrellas and whips, and during the 'Twenties, rose stockings and beaded and fringed skirts. Now the contents of the wardrobe had ceased to change: the Balcárcel's used, forever, the clothing of the 'Thirties. A double-breasted suit for him, with wide lapels and vest and a Scotch plaid tie. For her, dresses with long narrow skirts, high throats, pleats over the bust. Asunción's hair also reflected the style of the first years of her marriage, for it was undulating and drawn back.

"He can't talk," she replied. She kept her eyes down, and her fingers slowly twisted a fold of the curtain. "He's delirious, he says things that don't make sense. He's hurt, Jorge, his feet are bleeding . . . ay!" She suffocated a sudden sob that was born more of her words than of the unhappy condition of her nephew.

From the moment the servant had discovered Jaime outside the entrance and had run in crying that the boy had been killed, Balcárcel had decided to take advantage of this crisis to reaffirm his authority in the family. He did not really care about the boy's hurts. His wife's reaction affected him little more.

"No one needs to know anything about it," he said. "There has already been so much talk about the boy that people call him half crazy."

"Crazy? But he was attacked . . . !"

"Bah! His injuries are self-inflicted, that's obvious."

"Jorge . . . don't you think we ought at least to try to understand why? I mean, the child must be suffering in some way. We should try to understand and help him."

"There is nothing to understand. We simply have to watch him closer and prescribe stricter rules for his conduct. Did you know that he has been deceiving us? He has merely been pretending to go to confession. I asked Father Lanagorta and Father Obregón. He has not knelt in the confessional in over a year."

"But we take communion together every Friday!"

Balcárcel compressed his lips and tapped his belly. His face, ironical and at the same time outraged, waited for Asunción to grasp the full gravity of the boy's misbehavior. She dropped the curtains and walked to the center of the room.

"Satan has entered him," she said softly.

"I forbid you to make a drama of it," said her husband with self-satisfaction. "Neither you nor Rodolfo will see the boy until he is better and I have taken him personally to Father Obregón. Afterward, I shall have a very clear talk with him. Decidedly it is not with wishes that we will save him, but with sternness and energy. Understand me well, Asunción. The savings which I have accumulated with such effort will enable me to retire next year. Once we own the block of buildings along the Olla lake, we will have a fortune of more than a million pesos and a monthly income of ten thousand pesos. Your brother will leave us this house when he dies, and the store can be modernized and its profit multiplied. What I am saying is that Jaime, as our only heir, will someday, if he knows how to handle his means, be able to live very comfortably indeed. We are the best in Guanajuato, Asunción. We cannot permit our line to be extinguished and our fortune squandered by the foolish behavior of this youth. He is quite capable of giving everything away to beggars."

Asunción did not hear her husband clearly. Of his words she retained only those that seemed to tell of his sterility,

and it was these that raced back and forth across her eyes—
the retinas drenched in Jaime's blood—until suddenly she lost
her physical balance and reached an arm toward Balcárcel.
He went on talking. She moved toward him blindly. His
words came from far away, from a leaden quagmire. She embraced him, but could not silence him . . .

"And *Don* Chema Naranjo has well observed that if not
Jaime, then who is going to inherit my business? Do you
remember when we came home from London? Our life then
was very different from today. We have had to rebuild our
fortune from the bottom up. Now Jaime, thanks to our labor,
will have every opportunity. Hasn't Eusebio Martínez asked
and asked for him to lead the Youth Front? The boy can go
decidedly far, if we can just clear the cobwebs out of his
mind in time."

. . . She embraced as she would have liked to embrace
Jaime: she put her hands to his genitals and squeezed hard,
struggling against his infamous sterility, trying to find the
juices of his life. Balcárcel cried out in pain. She moved away
and fell on her back on the bed and began to mutter prayers
while she felt that an enormous black triangle was covering
her mouth, and the tongue of her delirium reached humid
and pink toward the lips of a blank face. She cried the Con-
fiteor and broke the seal of the story that had been locked in
so many years of a cold bed waiting for insemination, counting their love-making on the fingers of both hands, smelling
the heavy and aging slumber of the tranquil man who all
those years had laid so dully beside her, so rarely upon her.
But it was not her husband but Jaime that she was seeing
now. The two figures mixed, the blood of the youth flowed
into the body of the man, and Asunción muttered her prayer
without understanding it, while her soul lost itself in the
whirling and diffuse visions of her hysteria.

"Decidedly, the condition of our nephew has affected her,"
Balcárcel said to the doctor when Asunción freed her arms

from the bed clothes and woke, her skin as pale as the sheets.

"The sedative has worked well," said the physician before departing.

Balcárcel pulled his armchair near the head of the bed. Asunción did not dare to open her eyes. Her husband closed his as he prepared to spend the night sitting up beside her.

"*Put your arms around me.*"

"*Why have these disagreeable things happened, dear God? I am a good man. I could have been a brilliant man. I contented myself laboring to the end that nothing would be wanting in this home. Perhaps I have been a little severe at times. But I had to counterbalance Asunción and Rodolfo's softness. Every family must have a head.*"

"*Put your arms around me.*"

"*I have not worked for myself, but for the boy. A few sick fools may criticize me for having been harsh in my lending, but I detest prodigality and I have a tranquil conscience. Too easy credit is dangerous. How many families have I saved from ruin! But why am I thinking these thoughts. Enough, enough.*"

"*It would cost you nothing to embrace me.*"

"*There is, decidedly, no reason for things to turn out badly. Everything in life must be paid for. Why am I repaid with unrest and rebellion? If I could only talk with you, Asunción, if you could only understand me. You may think that I have at times been cold with you. But that is my way of showing respect. I will not bring prostitution into my home. I'm not perfect, I have the desires of any man. But you I respect: when I fall into temptation, I go to León or Guadalajara or Mexico City. In my home I am clean, and I love you chastely. Would you understand that if I told you? I have wanted to be a good man.*"

"*I won't say anything to you. But let there happen, please, just one moment of tenderness.*"

"*When Jaime grows up, he will understand matters. How*

*could we have let him be reared by his mother, a woman
whose life has proved her natural tendencies? She has ended
up a whore disguised as a mystic. And the fugitive the police
were after, the criminal. Why does that worry the boy so
much? I can understand that he should feel a natural affection for his mother, for he is too young to see her for what
she is. But the criminal! I obeyed the law and my own conscience when I turned the man in. May the boy soon grow
out of his damn adolescence! He is living a kind of sickness.
But by and by he will become a man, and will be all right.
I hope to see my pains with him recompensed some day . . .
if these quarrels don't kill me first."*

"*I'll never ask it of you again. Tomorrow will be like any
other day, and I will ask you nothing. All I want is for you
to come near and take me in your arms now. How long has
it been since you told me that you love me?*"

Balcárcel leaned toward her. Her cheeks were red, on a
face that was usually pale. She did not open her eyes.

"Do you feel better?"

Asunción nodded.

"I have decided to take Jaime to the priest tomorrow. He
can't go on as he is. It doesn't matter that he is sick. His real
sickness is of the soul, and it is the soul that must be treated."

Asunción nodded.

Balcárcel resumed his rigid posture. The velvet curtains,
the mahogany wardrobe, the piano of inlaid wood, the portraits on the walls, the enormous bed and his mosquito curtains, all had more life than the man and woman in the room.

When dawn began to filter through the curtains, Asunción
said:

"Why don't you lie down? I swear that I feel all right. You
won't bother me."

"Come, my son. It's a long time that you haven't confessed.
The church is big and cold, we don't have to stay here. First

we'll talk a little, in the sacristy. I'm glad to see you. Not since the Catechism, eh? My, how you've grown. Almost all your friends come to confess with me now."

Father Obregón passed his arm over Jaime's shoulders and noticed the boy's slight tremble. Jaime remembered the priest, he had instructed him when he was preparing for his First Communion. Afterward he had heard his schoolmates speak of Obregón's gentleness, above all compared with the malice of Lanzagorta. But until now the priest had been only a large black figure without face. Now, as they walked down the central aisle, Jaime observed him. He felt the priest's hand heavy on his shoulder. Father Obregón's breathing gave off the smell of tobacco. His black hair was combed forward in a careless fringe. The small black eyes were lost in the vigorous drawing of the eyebrows, the lashes, the prominent cheekbones, the thick eyelids. A little fuzz that would never really be a beard but that was never cleanly shaven covered his chin. But what most caught the boy's attention, as he lowered his eyes, were the sturdy shoes of scratched leather; the thick double soles, many times repaired, had with use and the dampness of the church taken a gondola shape that seemed to Jaime both strange and saintly. When they arrived in front of the altar, the man and the boy stopped and crossed themselves and executed a brief reverence. Obregón's cough resounded across the empty nave. Their steps left marble echoes. The priest opened the gate in the wooden grill which separated the altar from the sacristy.

Dampness had encrusted the high-ceilinged timbers of the sacristy, but the sensation was of warmth and richness. A great chest of blue tile and wood occupied the end of the room. There the ecclesiastical garments were kept. A chasuble with a yellow fringe had been laid on top of the chest. At the other end of the room was a baroque altar flowering with wreathes of entwined laurel and walnut leaves and plump angels. The gilded columns rose to the ceiling and continued across it in a painting of blue laurel and olive leaves strung upon a cordon; the Grecian fret continued around the room. Three walls shone with ostentatious richness; the fourth was naked white plaster broken by a tiny barred window that looked out on a gray alley. Father Obregón seated himself in a high wooden chair and invited the boy to take the other, smaller one.

"Why haven't you come to confess?" said the priest as he rubbed the boy's undulant blond hair.

"I didn't need to," said Jaime in a firm low voice. "I'm here now because they forced me to come."

"Forced you? No one can force you."

"Yes, they forced me. I have nothing to confess."

Obregón smiled and tapped his fingers on the richly carved arm of the chair. "For you I am merely another man, is that it?"

"I'm a man, too," the boy's tight lips replied.

"All of us are men. Our Lord was also a man, He suffered and died as a man."

Jaime lifted his face and challenged the priest: "Yes, that is why I can talk with Him. He can understand me and I can beg forgiveness without any need for anyone . . ."

Obregón slapped his hand down on the arm of the chair and stood up. The western sun gilded his face and the altar. "No, Jaime, no one can say that. Two men are always needed to approach God. One man alone can't do it. Do you understand me, you who are a man now? Alone you can't do it."

Was the boy only a child? Did he understand? His face was firm and raised, challenging. A shadow of doubt crossed his eyes. Jaime was remembering the words of Ezequiel Zuno. The priest's hand touched the boy's curly head again. The sun that is closest to man, the dying sun, shone upon them.

"How can I put it to you? I want you to understand, I don't want to force anything upon you. Have you ever prayed for others? Tell me: have you ever asked God to do something for someone else?" Obregón's voice became metallic and his hand fell heavily on the boy's shoulder. "Or have you challenged God the same way you challenge me? Have you merely offended him with your pride?" The priest began to pace, thinking of his next words.

"With my pride?" Jaime leaned forward. "Am I proud because I believe I must follow Christ's teachings just as He did?"

Obregón turned a flaming face: "You believe that you can equal Jesus Christ!"

"I believe that I can imitate Him."

"How can I cure you of this evil!"

"Don't shout at me."

"I'm listening, my son."

The boy's words were serene and calm. Hearing them, Father Obregón felt a deep tenderness. The ancient damp richly adorned sacristy was converted into a stage with two actors. But poor Father Obregón, who had been such an excellent seminarian, who had begun his ministry so well prepared, had gradually lost over the years, here in the provinces, the habit of dialogue. He felt himself weak inside, yet he had to find the right words. This boy who had come armed with insolence had at least the healthy confidence to believe what he said. How could his priest answer him? Answer him truly, not with the tired everyday phrases used with the simple pious people of his congregation. He felt that Jaime's challenge was not wholly invalid. And this made him feel first ashamed of himself and then deeply tender toward the boy. He spoke quietly:

"Before you say anything, let me tell you something. You are a man, yes, but you are still very young. Your sins can't be very great. They can't be very different from those of other young men like you. Have you ever stopped to think that there are thousands and thousands of young people who, just like you . . ."

Obregón felt that his words were wrong, that they were dictated by weakness instead of true love.

"Each of us has to do his penance," Jaime said coldly. Then, noticing the priest's anguished face, he went on: "Isn't that right, Father? What good does it do me to think that others may be worse than I am? I believe that I have my own special punishment, a penance that I have to do alone, as if I were . . . the only sinner in the world. When others don't realize that they have sinned, someone has to step for- ward and be penitent for them, doesn't he?"

"My son, my son, don't torture yourself in this way," said the priest with more certainty, drawing near the seated and motionless boy. "Understand that your sins are no more than the sins of your years. They can only be sins of love that has begun to search and so far has found only itself. That can't be evil, you must not think that it is evil. Later, when you have to decide whether you are going to love someone be- sides yourself, God and your wife, that is when we will know if you have done right or wrong. So many are so ashamed of their first love, their self-love, that afterward they don't dare offer it to others. And that is what is serious, my son. Tomor- row that will be your test: to learn to love others. That is why I want to help you, so your love will flow out without sorrow or desperation. To imitate Jesus! You ask the hardest task of all. If you fail, you die of hopelessness. That is why you must trust me, and understand that to come to God, you need my aid, or the aid of some other person."

"It doesn't matter if that other person is a very humble and poor man, or a woman who is a great sinner?"

"Christ came for them. But alone you can't do it, do you understand?"

"Yes," said Jaime. "Yes, I think I do." He smiled and kissed the priest's hand. "But, Father, I believe that everything you say, all that world of love, is possible for me only if I follow Christ's teaching."

"We all believe that, my son. And in order to follow His teaching, we need the Church, which is Christ's Body on earth. How can you go one way while the Church goes another?" Father Obregón tapped the stones of the floor with a heavy shoe.

"The Church isn't Christ any longer," said the boy harshly. "The Church is where *Doña* Asunción and Uncle Balcárcel and all the others come once a week in order to feel that they are decent. They come here as if they were going to a theater or a party, to be seen. Christ doesn't matter to them. They don't want to live like him, and what is more, they can't."

"Don't deny the possibility of goodness, don't judge others. That is hardly His teaching. Do you believe that your aunt and uncle, and your father, and all these good people, have committed great sins?"

"Yes, yes! They have all done much evil . . ."

"But it is not for you to punish them for the evil they have done, but what you must do is do good yourself."

The sun disappeared and the room was suddenly dark. For several seconds Obregón could not see Jaime, and he was about to call out when he felt the boy embrace him.

"Father," said the voice hidden in the priest's arms, "Can't we be what He wanted? Can't we forgive the evil in others, sacrifice everything in His name, assume as He did the guilt and the suffering of others, and lose ourselves in His heart? Why don't you yourselves follow him in everything? Why don't we all sacrifice as He did and live in humility and poverty? I am guilty, Father! Punish me, whip me!"

The boy sobbed in Father Obregón's arms, his nostrils full of the penetrating smell from the priest's armpits and the stink of his seldom-washed clothing.

"Compose yourself, my son. You tear my heart. Don't cry.

Listen to me." A thick dampness was seeping through the boy's shirt, staining the priest's hands, but Father Obregón did not notice. "I've spent fifteen years in my ministry. I am forty. Take my handkerchief, blow your nose, go on . . . In those fifteen years I have heard thousands of confessions. I admit it: sin is monotonous and unchanging. It is the same in everyone. Sometimes I think that my poor sinners hardly deserve absolution, for they don't sin seriously, and they don't merit a serious penance . . ."

"Punish me, Father! I want to know how much I can stand!"

"Jaime, compose yourself." He still did not feel the dampness on his hands from the boy's back. "We are merely humans, the best of us is mediocre. And it is for those who have confessed to me, ordinary people, it is for them that Christianity lives, not for exceptional beings. The saint is an exception. But religion is an everyday affair, for men and women of whom it cannot be asked, if we are charitable, anything fiery. How can we demand that they assume the sins of everyone?"

Jaime drew back. "You compromise! Christ doesn't love those who go halfway!"

The priest rose and a deep sigh escaped him. He walked to the big chest and lifted his cassock to look for the matches in his trousers. He lit two faint candles. "Saint Francis of Sales said that he served God in a human way and in accordance with his times, in the hope that some day he would be able to serve him in a divine way and in accordance with eternity."

The boy's weak voice, still strained from sobs: "And what is the human way?" In spite of the candles, his figure was invisible. Father Obregón blew out the match and a gray twist of smoke ascended nervously toward the ceiling.

"God wants us to be faithful in the little ways that His Providence has put within our reach. We are mortal, feeble, and we can do no more than fulfill the daily duties of our condition. There are great things which do not depend upon us. The sublime is far above us. We must content ourselves." The priest's voice, low and pious, sounded cavernous in the sacristy. "Your father, Jaime, is one of the little men God loves. You must not offend him, but must love him too."

"How do you know?" said Jaime, turning.

"I know. You must understand that you are no better or worse than all the rest, and that each of us in his own way fulfills the divine law. You call that compromise. I call it charity. Now go, it is late, and come back tomorrow and confess properly. It is late and I am tired."

Jaime kissed Obregón's hand and walked away. It was only then that the priest saw his full figure, the blue trousers and the white shirt, and realized that the boy was walking painfully, almost stumbling. Jaime reached the gate of the wooden grill and suddenly stopped and doubled over.

"I feel very sick, Father."

And only then did Obregón discover his own hands covered with blood. The boy was now walking slowly down the central aisle. Father Obregón suddenly understood and ran after him. He collapsed on his knees at the boy's feet. Lifting his face, he cried:

"Pray for me!"

Balcárcel observed the scene from the last pew in the church. When the priest fell to his knees, Balcárcel stopped playing with his watch-chain and started to step forward and make his presence known. But confusion paralyzed him.

Jaime reached the church door. His uncle tried to take his arm. The boy repulsed him and walked in front of him home along narrow dark blue streets where lampposts were just lighting, and the burned scent of spring rose from the paving stones.

Chapter 8

Jaime had not seen Juan Manuel since the night at Irapuato. Now spring vacation had begun and Jaime had fallen sick again, of fever. His convalescence was prolonged several weeks. He read novels, drank lemonade, and received long visits from his aunt. They did not speak of what had happened. Asunción knitted, with her bust very straight and her shoulders not touching the back of the chair.

"How time runs!" she commented. "Only yesterday Pascualina Barona's nephews were little boys, and this year they are going to graduate. Have you thought about what you will do when you finish preparatory? I hope you'll study law. Law was your father's golden dream, but the Revolution . . ."

Señorita Pascualina and *Doña* Presentación would drop by every afternoon. Jaime would close his book and his eyes.

"Is he sleeping?"

"Poor child! A boy that age is the Calvary of parents!"

"Don't worry, Asunción, we haven't told anyone. We've said that he has diphtheria."

"What would people say if they knew he had gone out into the mountains to flagellate himself!"

"He'll soon grow up now. It will all pass."

118

Then the two women would relate the week's religious happenings to Asunción, who because of her attendance upon Jaime was unable to go out, and tell of conversations with Father Lanzagorta and comment upon last Sunday's sermon.

Balcárcel never entered Jaime's room. Rodolfo did, however, and his presence irritated Jaime more than anyone's. He would recognize his father's slow step in the corridor and immediately close his eyes. Rodolfo would draw near the bed and grip its gilded rungs, and although he knew the boy was pretending, stand there for a long time. Behind his closed eyes, Jaime was cold and hostile; he wanted Rodolfo to feel that he was now being paid in his own coin for his rejection of Adelina. Against this bitterness was opposed the hope that his father would go find her and help her, the wonderful act of manhood and honesty that would allow Jaime to love him again.

Rodolfo understood well enough that he had lost his son's affection. He did not know why. He thought again and again, sadly now, of their happy times together a few years ago. Rodolfo's life had become rutted and empty. Weekdays he attended the clothing store, where business was always a little worse today than it had been yesterday. Boredom took him to double-feature Mexican motion pictures in the evenings. Sunday mornings he drank beer in the Jardín del Unión with his old friends. Saturday nights he crept out of the house and went to a bordel, where a short brown-skinned girl with a mole on her forehead expected him at ten exactly. His visits with her were quick and silent, only the essential words were spoken, they had never exchanged names. He always noticed how she looked away when he laboriously unhooked his suspenders and dropped his trousers. When he left her, the next man would already be waiting in the hall. Then he would walk slowly home, at eleven in the evening, to the stone mansion.

Jaime improved and one day dared to ask Asunción if his friend Juan Manuel had been to see him. His aunt said no.

"Haven't you learned your lesson yet? You have to begin to think about what lies ahead of you. Dedicate yourself to your studies and forget your peasant friend and your crazy ideas. You see how I've managed to calm down your uncle; he even lets you read anything you want to now."

"Hasn't Father Obregón come either?"

"Yes, he came. He said that you are to wait a while before you go to see him again, and that you must remember well what he told you. I don't know . . . sometimes I think there must be something strange, something soft about Father Obregón. All the schoolboys like him so much, there must be some reason. Don't you want to go back to Father Lanzagorta?"

"No . . . no."

"As you wish. We'll see what your uncle says."

"I would like to see Juan Manuel."

"Haven't you learned your lesson yet?"

The first days of May, Rodolfo Ceballos began to decline. First he felt a growing weariness as he climbed to his room. He would have to stop and rest at least four times. The servants of the house, accustomed to the iron clatter, were frightened listening to how slowly he moved. Four, five steps, his hands gripping the circular steel railing; it seemed that the feeble structure could not support the weight of his heavy body. Then he would climb a little higher and rest again while looking about him with an expression of alarm.

Next he began to find it hard to sleep. He could be heard pacing the roof at night. "You'll get pneumonia," said Asunción. One of the small rewards for his insomnia, however, was the pleasure of watching dawn rise. The thin air made him cough. Then a pale white feather would rise on an horizon that a moment before had been opaque and glassy.

At six in the morning he would go back to bed and sleep half an hour. A strange dream troubled him: he felt that the bedroom was full of enemies and that he was at the bottom of a well, and the harder he struggled to escape, the more helpless, defenseless, and groggier he became. He woke a little before seven and went down to breakfast: a sweet roll and a cup of tea. His lower belly tightened with pain. He excused himself and in the bathroom urinated, painfully and with difficulty. He urinated frequently, so often that the chamberpot in his bedroom was insufficient and he would have to stand over the roof drainpipe.

A mania for collecting family pictures came over him. He searched trunks in the old stable, drawers of the roll-top desk Uncle Pánfilo had used; he even asked Asunción for photographs of herself, of Balcárcel, and of the boy. The yellow walls of his bedroom were covered with these pictures, some of them old and stained and dull, others glossy and new. They comforted and entertained him strangely. Secretly he believed that the familiar faces would frighten away the faceless enemies who surrounded him in his dream. At times he realized that something deeper and more elemental was happening in his life. He would sit for hours in his sagging armchair, staring at the family paraded across his walls. There, an engraving of Grandfather Higinio, with clear steady eyes. There, his mother Guillermina, her head twisted in the least comfortable of poses. In the oval of that daguerreotype she was the young Guillermina, with ringlets over her ears and a cluster of carnations at her bodice. Above the head of the bed Rodolfo hung a sepia photograph of his mother and father on their wedding day, both very wide-eyed, she in a long-trained gown, he with blond beard and a stiff shirt; behind them a painted curtain representing the Rialto Bridge and the Grand Canal in Venice. Other photographs were less elegant. The only one of Adelina showed a thin smiling girl seated on a garden bench. She wore a black sheath in the style of the 'Twenties and her knees were exposed. A beaded ribbon encircled her forehead. In another photograph, Rodolfo himself smiled, one hand holding a fishing pole and the other touching the head of a little boy with a candy sucker.

Rodolfo even went so far, without in the least knowing why, as to exhume the old lithograph of *Don* Porfirio Díaz. And when he seated himself in his armchair and contemplated the faces on his walls, he felt himself near something warm and unchanging.

He lost weight. Garments that had been tight on a man of ninety-six kilos hung loosely about him; he had to begin using a belt to gather the folds of his trousers around his waist. His neck emerged wrinkled and skinny from his too-large collars. He vomited often, and then began to pass blood in his urine.

"Decidedly, Rodolfo has gone on a diet in order to marry again," Balcárcel remarked in a rare moment of humor. And Asunción said to Rodolfo as he finished breakfast one morning: "You! The servants know what you do at night . . . it runs down the drain into the patio!" Only Jaime did not speak to him. Nevertheless it was only to Jaime that Rodolfo directed his loving, pleading gaze.

His attempts to establish closeness with his son intensified daily, as if he realized that he had very little time left in which to consummate the one love of his life. His sick smile was fixed upon the boy through every meal. Well might Balcárcel fume and raise his eyebrows about the peculiar behavior of certain members of the family at certain times, well might Asunción glance nervously; the elder Ceballos simply sat there staring mutely at his son. Jaime pretended not to notice, and kept his head down. But one night, while Balcárcel was orating as always—his subject was the treasonable Jacobism of the Juaristas—Jaime could not stand his father's stare any longer and jumped to his feet, throwing his napkin down, and exclaimed:

"Please, Aunt, tell him not to look at me this way!"

"What's this? What sort of behavior is this?" said Balcárcel, so rudely interrupted and suddenly suspicious that no one had been paying him the slightest attention. "Decidedly, this is going too far! Sit down and eat your dinner. I shall now repeat the essence of my remarks about Jacobism. And you, Rodolfo, who seem to be the cause of this scene, what do you have to say for yourself, sir? I trust you agree that someone must be in authority in this house, and I do not see how *you. . .*"

Rodolfo's paralyzed smile did not change. He continued staring intensely at the nervous boy.

"I am addressing you, sir!"

"Jorge, he's sick," said Asunción, excusing her brother with the truth that none of them had until this moment dared to utter. The truth: the thing that was forbidden among them. She realized her mistake and dropped her eyes.

"Sick!" said Balcárcel between his teeth. "No one is sick here. We are a little tired and nervous, that's all. We will have no more talk about sickness." He sought, for a moment, some way to censure her, and finding none, rose and with his knuckles upon the tablecloth announced that he would take his coffee in the library.

The opalescent light fell upon the three silent figures at the green table. Asunción and Jaime tried to avoid Rodolfo's fixed eyes and unaltering smile. The father swallowed the boy with his stare. Jaime lowered his head and with a murmur excused himself and left the dining room.

The brother and sister did not speak. They listened to Jaime's steps on the stone of the hall. Then the rigid ticking of the old clock in the drawing room. They sat just outside the circle of light, with their heads bent slightly. Evening's dampness began to descend from the beamed ceiling and the papered walls. Rodolfo extended a hand splotched with brown spots and veined with gray, and toyed with a spoon.

"How different . . ." he said softly.

"What?" Her brother's face had a look of finality, as if his features had come to their last definition and would never change again.

"How different we are from what we could be."

Her posture rigid, a black statue of angular curves, she listened and heard. She wanted to understand Rodolfo, now that Jaime was becoming a man and was escaping both of them. But she knew, without daring to think it, that to understand was the same thing as to hurt: truth was cruel.

"Why haven't we been like papá and mamá?" Rodolfo's phlegmed voice was saying. "Why haven't we been as happy as they were? Did you ever know them to have a quarrel? We were so affectionate and loving with them, we were one family . . . And how papá used to play with us! What a fine old man he was, and how cheerful!"

"Do you remember the puppets he gave me for my ninth birthday?"

"Of course I do, of course I do!" Rodolfo's fingers tapped the velvet tablecloth. "He liked to make others happy, that was why he was always so happy himself. But you and I . . ."

"We have done what was possible for us, Rodolfo. Not everything has been so bad."

"But the point is that everything could have been so beautiful. If I could have found a woman like mamá, my son could have been mine . . . And if you could have had a child of your own, you wouldn't have wanted to take him away from me. He would have been mine."

From the table rose an unpleasant scent of abandoned plates, congealing grease. Asunción stood beside her brother and put her arm around him. "You're sick, Fito. You don't really know what you're saying."

"Oh, I know. I know that I was left by myself, that Adelina

was taken away from me, everything that could make life warm and give me companionship now, and that all of you are going to let me die alone in my room . . ."

"Rodolfo!" She had to support him or he would have toppled from the chair. "Rodolfo!" she repeated, embracing a figure that had lost its bone. His head fell forward on the table. "I warned you against that woman, didn't I? I told you that she was unworthy of you and our family. Now, today, you know it yourself, for she has found her destiny. You were stupid, stupid. If I had been here, none of it would have happened! She was trash, just a glance at her was enough to tell you that. All she wanted was your name, your money, she didn't love you."

"She didn't love me?" said the voice suffocated upon the tablecloth. "I don't know . . . Yes! Yes, she loved me! And at least I had someone I could love. We all need someone to love, even if we aren't loved in return."

"She didn't love you at all! You knew it was impossible for her to be Jaime's mother. That was why I had to be the mother, because you had made a fool of yourself. It was all your own fault."

Her words spat out over an inert and wrinkled face. The flood of thoughts that for years had been held back gave her a sense of release and strength. But Rodolfo no longer wanted to listen. He wanted to sleep, to rest. With a movement of his hand he asked her to help him stand.

"Take me upstairs. I feel sick."

Then they heard a sound from the drawing room. Jaime came in and helped his father up. Rodolfo pressed his head against the boy's chest and with closed eyes moved his lips to kiss his shirt.

Only once more did Jaime see his father dressed and on his feet. He watched from a window as Rodolfo came down the street, and he thought, that is my father: that yellow figure, those hanging clothes, that shrunken face, those bulging bloodshot empty eyes. Rodolfo very slowly climbed to the drawing room, washed his hands in the ornate basin in the dining room, and before he sat at the table, said that he was short of breath. His plate of puréed vegetables—all that he could swallow without pain—grew cold. Asunción was rolling her husband's napkin into its polished silver ring, and paid little attention. "Come now, something hot will be good for you." Jaime watched his father and expected the sick eyes to stare imploringly at him again. But Rodolfo was too weak for that now. He slowly staggered across the room, and Jaime sat motionless and observed his physical collapse. Rodolfo stopped, holding to a lapis-lazuli column; he closed his eyes and breathed deep, and walked into the hall. Later they found him stretched on Jaime's bed. He had not had strength enough to climb to the roof. The doctor ordered that he was not to be moved. Jaime slept on the leather sofa in the library, for the room on the roof filled him with disgust. "But if there's nothing contagious . . ." said *Doña* Asunción. "And we can put your sheets on the bed."

Every morning of the three weeks of life that remained to Rodolfo, Jaime would enter the bedroom to get fresh clothes. The conversation between his father and his aunt that he had overheard pleased him. But when he came into his father's dying presence, he did not know what to say or how to draw near him. Day's first pale light bathed the sick man's drawn skull. He was ugly, a wretched and ugly old man with a gaping smile and gummed eyelids. His uncombed hair fell over his ears. Jaime pulled open a drawer to choose a shirt, and tried to choose a word for his father too. But then he lifted his face and saw himself in the mirror, young, healthy, with clean-cut features and blond fuzz above his lips. He never found a word. Nor did his father speak to him. They waited.

A few days before he died, Rodolfo gathered all his

strength and stretched his arms and took his son's hand. Jaime sat beside him and felt repelled by the stench of sickness and the dirty green-striped pajamas. Rodolfo's flabby neck, his gray beard and his shoulders trembled with a strange desire. His still-living cadaver wanted to speak to Jaime, and he tried to pull the boy's head near his lips. But the gray tongue moved without words. Jaime's eyes dropped. He thought of the Bible verse about a house divided against itself. He and his father were forever separated from each other now. Jaime was youth, life. Rodolfo was death. Neither wanted to know his opposite. Jaime did not hear the words that finally struggled from his father's bubbling throat: "We don't live long . . . We die a long, long time." The doctor knocked. Jaime welcomed the interruption, and stood up. But he returned to the bed, obeying a clear impulse, and squeezed his father's hand.

Asunción woke at four. The crowing of cocks accompanied her weeping. It was a blue dawn, and in its light Rodolfo's stiff face was like metal. His hands held a crucifix. Jaime stood in the door and thought: he has died in the room of my youth, on the bed of my seventeen years. He tried to suffocate the sob that escaped through his nose and mouth. Now his father—those blue hands, that white sheet—had no name.

Uncle Balcárcel remained standing with his hand nailed to his vest. He had assumed his most somber face. Asunción was on her knees weeping. Father Obregón rose from the head of the bed and said in a low voice: "We always come too late." As he passed Jaime, he looked at him with severity. "Come to see me day after tomorrow."

"*Requiem aeternam dona eis, Domine,*" Asunción was murmuring.

Balcárcel stepped out into the hall and arched his eyebrows: "Late or soon, it comes to all of us."

Now his father, Jaime was thinking, had no name; a last

gesture of love was impossible, the word he had begged of him every day during these weeks. He felt like going to the body and kissing the forehead. But the feeling that he would be acting a lie held him back. He stood in the door and wished that he could speak to the shrunken figure on the bed, and ask forgiveness for his pride and youth.

"Decidedly, he was a good man," pronounced Balcárcel. "Badly disciplined, yes. But a good man."

". . . *et lux perpetua luceat eis . . .*"

The man from the funeral parlor arrived at six in the morning.

"A hopeless case: cancer of the stomach," said the doctor. Then he asked all of them to leave the bedroom.

Chapter 9

SPADES FULL OF EARTH began to fall on the coffin. Bitter happiness flooded Jaime's chest and he felt a sense of liberation he could not understand. It had rained for several days and the coffin seemed to float in the clayey depth like a caravel ready to set sail as soon as the mourners departed.

"Please deport yourself well," Asunción had said to the boy. "This is the first time you have had to attend the funeral of a member of the family. Put on one of your uncle's black ties, and stand in line beside us."

There he stood now, giving his hand to *Don* Chema Naranjo, to *Doña* Presentación Obregón and to *Señorita* Pascualina, to decrepit Uncle J. Guadalupe Montañez, to powerful *Señor* Maximino Mateos, to the Daughters of Mary, to Father Lanzagorta. Their compunctious faces and their squeezed fists and their words of consolation were all the same. Jaime moved his head restlessly. None of these people had ever taken the hand of Rodolfo Ceballos during his life. The fat merchant had been, at most, a reason for some forgotten gossip. No one had taken his hand, the boy reflected as he received the last *abrazo* of condolence, and he, his son, least of all.

"May I stay here alone for a few minutes?" he asked his aunt and uncle when the file of mourners reached the exit to the cemetery. Balcárcel shrugged his shoulders. "Don't be long," whispered Asunción. "Your uncle has an important business meeting tonight and won't be home. Please have dinner with me."

Jaime walked along the cypress-lined footpath, hurrying his steps, intentionally shouldering the lowest branches. Dampness speckled his face.

One figure remained beside the grave where Rodolfo Ceballos lay. It was Juan Manuel Lorenzo, strange in his blue suit. The two friends shook hands.

"I waited until the others left, Ceballos."

"Thank you, Lorenzo."

"I came to see you while you were sick. Did they give you my messages?"

"No."

They walked back. Each knew that the other would not break the silence. From the distant hills, a leaden sky was rushing swiftly over Guanajuato. In the twilight the city's vapors said farewell once again to day. Carpenter's varnish pots, fumes from blacksmiths' shops, the faint smokes of slum chimneys. Church bells were clanging, the bells of mules tinkled counterpoint. Under silver clouds, the colonial domes, blue walls of winding streets, white villages that clung to the sides of the steep valleys.

"I waited for you . . . the day after we were at Irapuato . . . so we could go and work together," said Juan Manuel as they started down the abrupt slope.

Jaime loosened his black tie and unbuttoned his collar. "You know something? That woman they called Fina . . ."

"She's your mother, Ceballos."

Jaime kicked a bottle-cap. "How did you know?"

"I've known a long time. She always said so . . . and she always comes to that bar."

"Why didn't you tell me?"

"Wasn't it better for you to learn yourself? Why didn't you tell her who you are, Jaime?"

"Is that what you would have done?"

"Yes. I wouldn't have felt ashamed."

"I wasn't ashamed!"

"Yes, you too . . . you felt ashamed of her, just like your father and your aunt and uncle."

"Juan Manuel. Juan Manuel."

They stopped. The damp field gathered with full hands all the deepest scents of the earth. For the first time the young friends had called each other by their first names.

Asunción waited for Jaime until nine. Dinner grew cold on the velvet tablecloth. Her solitary and motionless figure at the head of the table was like one of the high-backed chairs. There were twelve chairs: *Don* Pepe Ceballos had had a large family and frequent guests. Family of eight in the epoch of the founder *Don* Higinio. Ten during Pepe's regency: Guillermina, the two children, the brother Pánfilo, the penniless Lemus relations, the Andalusian grandmother *Doña* Margarita, and Asunción's fiancé. And now she was there alone, without her husband, without Jaime.

At nine she asked for a cup of warm chocolate. Afterward she wrapped herself in her woolen shawl and slowly walked the length of the drawing room, stopping to look through the curtains of each balcony. A fine mist had begun to fall like cobweb threads. She straightened the portrait of Governor Muñoz Ledo. She descended to the patio and climbed the spiral iron stairs to the room that still smelled of her brother. One by one she took down the pictures of the family he had collected during his last months.

She left the room and locked the door. She thought of the house in its best times, when there were ten servants, when every room had been occupied and the stable full of horses and carriages.

With the pictures in her arms she went down and walked to the front corridor. Not for a long time had she visited the stable. She laid the pictures on top of a trunk. Her heel ground the wings of a dry butterfly. She looked down: her butterfly collection. She had made it when she was thirteen. It had been her passion, she had even carried the glass-topped cases with her on vacation trips. She squatted and picked up the crushed wings. Bright blue and black still glistened through accumulated dust. She caressed the wings tenderly.

And now, as she remembered her adolescent hobby, it came to her for the first time that the future offered her nothing.

When she left the stable, she locked it too.

Rain made their coats shine. The drizzle had begun about seven but they didn't mind it, they were used to walking bareheaded under that eternal fine mist. Now they blew away the spume of their fifth beer, and laughed. They had never before drunk so much; the alcohol did not seem to affect Juan Manuel, but Jaime was waving his arms and passing his hand over his damp uncombed hair. He had heard that when you are drunk, everything reels. His sensation was that the walls and the objects hung upon them had separated and were throwing themselves at his head.

". . . and all the time there was that baboon Mateos trying to scare the girls with his dirty tricks," said Jaime, palming his friend's shoulders. "Have you ever confessed?"

Juan Manuel shook his head.

"You do right. Or maybe you do wrong. But that buzzard Father Lanzagorta, the things he told me . . . the things he told me! Say, Manuel! Have you ever been to bed with a woman?"

Again Juan Manuel shook his head.

"Well, let's do it! You got money? I don't either."

Jaime took off his wristwatch.

"How much will you give me?" he asked the man behind the bar.

"To pay what you owe?"

"No, we have enough for that, sure we have enough."

"That's different. A hundred pesos."

"It's worth five hundred."

"No."

"A hundred and what we owe."

"Good."

"Take it. Where can we find some women? The best place . . ."

"There's a good house very near here."

"Let's go."

"Tell them I sent you."

"Sure. Thanks."

Again they were walking through the drizzle. Jaime felt good; he even tried to sing. He embraced Juan Manuel, he clung to his friend's unswaying body.

"Happy, that's how I feel!"

"You're . . ."

". . . *subí a la palma, palmero . . .*"

"You're glad to be alive."

Jaime laughed. "You see everything, don't you? All the way to the bottom of my soul!"

The bordel door was not opened quickly.

"All the girls are busy right now. If you will step into the living room and have a drink . . ."

A juke-box was blaring a rhumba and the hall was in shadow. From the living room came a great racket of partying. The small bedrooms opened on the hall, which was lined with flower-pots. Out of one of the doors stepped a short

brown-skinned girl with a mole on her forehead. She fastened
her blouse. She saw Jaime and took his arm.

"Why go any farther?"

"Sure, this is far enough."

"A hundred pesos."

"I can only give you fifty, *señorita*. I have to pay for my
friend too."

"All right."

Then the beer went away and Jaime realized that he was
afraid. He was trembling uncontrollably. He breathed on his
hands. All he could say was: "How cold it is!"

She asked him if this would be the first time, and he ad-
mitted it.

"What's your name?"

"Ro. . . Rodolfo. What's yours?"

"Olga."

The girl snapped the light off.

When he left her, Jaime shouted for Juan Manuel and his
friend answered from another room. The noise from the
living room continued. He had been with the girl only ten
minutes.

"Don't you smoke?" she said when she came out into the
hall. Jaime said that he didn't.

"Come on, let's go in the living room for a few minutes
so you can see what it's like. And remember, I'm here every
day except Sunday."

They walked down the dark hall. The living room was at
the back. Olga spread the door curtains and put an arm
around Jaime's neck. A group of men and women were dancing and laughing. On the sofa, seated with an air of presiding
over the party, was *Don* Maximino Mateos. And atop a small
table with his shoes and his coat off and his armpits splotched
with sweat and a crepe-paper hat on his balding head, Uncle
Jorge Balcárcel was dancing all alone, dancing all alone with
a bottle of rum hugged in his arms. Everyone was laughing,

but Jaime laughed harder than all of them. The girl beside him doubled over with laughter too.

Balcárcel saw Jaime and was paralyzed.

Jaime kissed the mouth of the girl with the mole on her forehead, and left the house.

Chapter 10

H<small>E SLEPT</small> until eleven: because of his father's death
he was excused from school and his aunt did not dare that
day to enter his bedroom. Balcárcel rose earlier than usual
and breakfasted alone. Asunción hardly had time to tell him
that Rodolfo's novena would begin in the evening.

In the afternoon Jaime went to see Father Obregón. The
priest met him at the foot of the main altar and with a curt
nod motioned him into the sacristy. There they sat as before,
Obregón on the high-backed elaborately carved chair, Jaime
on the small plain one. But this time no hint of self-doubt
or expression of tenderness escaped the priest.

"I want to confess," Jaime smiled, anxious to tell a confessor for the first time that he had been with a woman.

When he finished, Obregón's badly-shaven face flamed.

"And to think I had faith in you, that I believed you were
one chosen by Our Lord. Yes: I believed you were a boy set
apart, capable of forgiveness and charity!"

Jaime suddenly felt a part of himself die. But he did not
understand: he thought the priest was referring to last night,
to the fact that he had gone to a bordel the same day his
136

father was buried. He tried to speak, but Father Obregón silenced him:

"I confessed your father the last day he was up and about and again the night he died. He wanted nothing in life except your love. He did not want to die without it. But you wouldn't give it to him, you were incapable of a single gesture. You condemned him to die in pain and desperation. You are a coward, do you understand me! A coward! You have sinned against the spirit, you have . . ."

"Father . . ."

The priest's fury mounted his face in red waves.

"And you dared to come here, full of pride, and talk about the Imitation of Christ, the true love of Our Lord! You, who could not give one whisper of love to your own father! You love no one except yourself. For others you show only pride in disguise. You are one more Pharisee!"

"Father, please, listen to me."

Obregón slapped the arm of his chair. "No, I shall not let you go on deceiving me with words. *You* listen, and pay attention. One day you went out into the mountains and harmed yourself physically. . ."

Again Jaime felt the priest's hot hands on his bleeding shoulders the afternoon Balcárcel had brought him, against the doctor's advice, to confess. He felt the biting lash of cactus thorns across his chest. He had lacerated his body as an act of penance for Balcárcel's self-satisfied face, for Aunt Asunción's frustration, for his father's timorous lack of manhood, for the horror of his mother in the dirty bar in Irapuato. He had made himself suffer in their names, to pay their guilt: one agonizing cut for forgiveness for Balcárcel, another for charity for Asunción, another for Rodolfo's weakness; and all for the sin committed upon his mother, solitary and abandoned. Pain for her pain . . .

"I know what you think: that it was an act of heroism, a penance to wipe away the evil done by others. . . ."

"Yes! I did it for my mother, I swear it. . . ."

"Bah! It was a foolish act lacking in faith, an act of hope-lessness, understand that. You merely wanted to punish your own sense of guilt. The only valid penance does not judge others. The only valid penance assumes the guilt of others from love alone, and does not expect recompense. What did *you* expect, you child? Some tangible result? A miracle in exchange for your pain?"

"Yes, yes. . . . I had faith. . . ."

"That men would change their habits between night and morning simply because you had felt agony? That thanks to you, human nature itself would change? You could be that proud! And that cowardly!"

"What should I have done, Father?"

"You should have had the guts to bend down to that unhappy abandoned woman your mother, and told her who you are and given her your love. That's what you should have done. And you should have given your father your love. Instead you piled offense upon offense. You have done nothing for no one."

"What must I do now?"

"Find your mother and love her truly, just as she is and for what she is. Don't go on offending God with your hatreds. Love the people around you, your aunt and uncle, and love them more the harder it is. And believe me it is harder by far than to cut your back and shoulders with a whip. Help them, stop hating them."

"Help them?"

"Yes, by loving them. That is your duty."

"How?"

"Without saying one word. Love them! Love them in spite of all the harm you feel they have done you. Listen to me clearly now: love is not words but deeds. You have come to me with words, but you have never been capable of a single act of true love. And your cowardice hurts me, for I had faith in you . . ."

With the face of a crying child, Jaime lowered his head. Who was Obregón to talk to him like this? Cassocked eunuch who had castrated himself voluntarily, who did not know true male passions. As he flushed with shame before the priest's accusations, the image of a woman's naked body in his arms filled his eyes. Abruptly he got up and ran out of the sacristy.

Father Obregón covered his face with his hands.

"My God, have I done good or evil? No one ever brings me real problems, the sins of my poor flock are so monotonous and simple that I have lost the habit of facing real problems. Have I helped this boy by telling him the truth? Or have I hurt him? Have I strengthened his faith, or broken it, my God?"

But when he sat to supper, his hot chocolate persuaded him that he had spoken well, very well. He had never before had the opportunity to do so, to show that his studies in the Seminary had not been in vain. Good. Good. . .

Jaime's troubled spirit welcomed the quiet of the novena. He kneeled beside Aunt Asunción and closed his eyes. Immediately he forgot the presence of Father Lanzagorta grasping the pulpit like a lion pawing the bars of its cage. He ceased to hear the singsong chant of the *Pater Noster* and the *Ave Maria,* the *Requiem Aeternam* and the *Ora pro nobis.* With a shamed look, Balcárcel slipped into the pew, but Jaime did not notice. He withdrew from his aunt and uncle, from the friends who had come to pray for the eternal rest of his father. He was alone with the black-skinned Christ of his adolescence, the twisted tortured image that tonight was speaking to him as during the Holy Week four years ago when he had awakened from boyhood:

"Do I have a destiny of my own, Lord?"

"You are not alone in the world, my son."

"Lord, I do not want to continue to deceive myself. I believed that I could be a good Christian, obeying your teachings . . . yes, alone in the world."

"But you are not alone and my teachings can be obeyed only beside others."

"Lord, I confess to you in secret that I will not be brave enough to stoop down to my mother. She and her life fill me with horror. I won't know what to say to her. And I cannot stand her words to me, her filth, her cheapness. Nor the way these people here tonight will talk about me . . ."

"Your best friend is an humble peasant boy."

"Lord, I confess in secret that I am Juan Manuel's friend only because it eases my conscience, just as I felt better that night I pretended to go work beside him at Irapuato."

"You feel that you are doing him a favor. You do not really love him."

"No . . ."

"You feel he is far beneath you, yet you can stretch your hand down to him with dignity. But to humiliate yourself by going to your mother would be too much, for then you would really belong to those beneath you. You would be one of them yourself. And you can love only from above."

The silver eyes of Christ nailed themselves to Jaime's.

"Lord, what must I do?"

"Whosoever wants to save his life, must lose it; and he who loses his life for my sake shall save it."

The voice of Christ faded, drowned by the Ora pro nobis:

> *Arc of David,*
> *Arc of the Covenant,*
> *Health of the sick,*
> *Morning star . . .*

His eyes opened. He looked at his aunt on his right. She

bent her head and chanted the litany. Uncle Balcárcel's gaze was fixed on the pulpit. Jaime did not lie to himself: to have seen Balcárcel in the whorehouse last night had been a pleasant victory. He would never reproach him again. He would accept him as he was, a hypocrite, weak, a Pharisee, a human.

Returning home, Jaime walked slowly to let the silent figures of his aunt and uncle draw ahead. Self-satisfaction and disgust battled within him. He felt a tense uneasiness which refused to be overcome. The Balcárcels were distant now. He did not want to be like them; nevertheless, what secure calm he felt when he thought of himself as part of them. He saw himself taller, stretching a long shadow below the street lamps. He put his hands in his pockets, shrugged his shoulders in a peculiar way, walked with a step that although slow was confident. He did not know it, but he was assuming now new attitudes which would accompany him the rest of his life. His face imitated characteristic expressions of his uncle and of *Don* Maximino Mateos. His smile was very like that of presidential candidate Alemán, whose placard picture covered the alley walls.

No: he was Jaime Ceballos, a youth walking home from church, from his father's novena to dinner, with his forehead creased by a very recent frowning line, with his head moving in an alert decisive way which concealed his hidden fears, with eyes that had lost their ability to be astonished and were ready to accept now without questioning, surprised only that there was no longer any mystery.

A moment of decision had passed. He had lifted his head in feeble challenge, only to give up challenges and become another conforming youth obedient to the unwritten law according to which youth must look about itself callously, indifferent to good and evil in the world.

The moment passed unnoticed. He felt only the silent

struggle, in the secret depth of his conscience, between disgust and self-satisfaction.

As he climbed the interlaced alleys, his thighs beginning to ache, he thought: how different everything has turned out to be. On the one hand the complex theorems of love and sin, man's fall and salvation; on the other life's vulgar plain reality: to fornicate, to conform to class and breeding, to die. He told himself that he had been stupid. Once that was what Pepe Mateos had called him: stupid asshole! as they were leaving school; and he had stood there, convulsed but silent, his fists tight, his face red, trembling, unable to reply, unable to give voice to what was inside him, the mystery of his adolescence and his adolescent ideas. Now he reflected that Pepe Mateos had been right. Yes: he had been the stupid asshole baby who had believed that every moment of life waited for you, to be enjoyed for itself alone and to offer every act a final value. And life was not like that. Life hurried, it never waited; today you were thrown into the transient arms of a whore, tomorrow you watched a man led off by the police, the next day you were drunk in a bar, and the last day you lay in your coffin. Pepe Mateos was right; Uncle Balcárcel was right: you come to the world only to fill up the time that is given you with quick words and thoughtless action.

He was within a block of the house. He slowed down. Unconsciously he had already decided to adopt a new attitude during the evening meal. He wanted to think of himself as already grown old, old as Balcárcel, or his own father, Jaime Ceballos, age fifty, standing behind a store counter or seated at a desk heaped with papers. Himself, but still the hero of his own adventure, which had not after all abandoned him: still the man who wished to lose himself in identification with the poor and humble and with the greatest words of the Christian spirit.

A chasm of solitude down the stone street. His aunt and

uncle had left the high front gate open, and through it suddenly appeared *Doña* Asunción's gray cat. A hot lump formed in Jaime's stomach. As on Easter Sunday four years ago, he sat down to let the cat press warm and sensual against his legs. The small soft body rubbed back and forth, its closed eyes showing blind pleasure in the friction and the affection.

He could never have explained why with abrupt decision and with actions so sure of themselves, he picked up the stone that held the gate open, raised it and smashed it down on the cat's head. There was a dry moan. The round silvery eyes filled with terror and supplication. With the heel of his shoe Jaime suffocated the sound; he forced down until the legs of the cat raised rigidly and a slight tremor bristled its soft gray hair. And so they remained for a long time, the standing boy, the dying cat, joined by open eyes and flowing blood.

Instinctively he moved toward the house. He walked backwards, his eyes hypnotized by the dead animal. To whom could he tell what he had done? With whom could he free his conscience? He sucked his finger and told himself that it was only a cat, that to kill a cat is not serious. He wanted to justify himself, to believe that he had been free to kill the cat. That his freedom was the reward that had been won by the youth who had flagellated himself and taken upon his own conscience the sins of others and made his soul Christ's abode.

He would have liked to be able to vanish into the solid stone wall. He slunk along the shadows of the corridor. His head danced as his thoughts unwrapped like the layers of skin of an onion, endlessly.

He ran in a circle and banged the gate shut. There, with his head pushed against the green wood, he prayed to be like everyone, anyone. He prayed to a new God far different from the God of his first youth, to be saved from the extremities of love and pride, sacrifice and crime, which joined in a single word of terror spoken in front of a dead cat.

He opened his eyes.

The important thing was to hide the body. He edged the gate open and peeped to see if the street was empty. He stretched his hand and caught the cat's tail. As the animal was dragged over the stone, it left a red streak. Jaime took out his handkerchief and wrapped it around the crushed head. He picked the cat up in his arms and ran to the patio and let it fall into the fountain. He washed his hands while the soggy body slowly disappeared.

He wadded his handkerchief and put it in his pocket. It was time for dinner. He climbed the stairs with confident steps.

Balcárcel made no moral pronouncements during the meal that night. Jaime's lips maintained a faint smile. His uncle was conquered. He had freedom now, he could speak at the table as he pleased, he could go and come when he chose; Balcárcel would never again oppose him. Asunción looked strangely at her husband, then at Jaime. The meal passed in silence. Jaime felt the sodden wad of the handkerchief in his pocket.

"I've decided to enter Law School next year," he announced when the dessert was served.

"Jaime, how wonderful!" cried Asunción, leaning over to kiss his forehead.

"*Don* Eusebio Martínez," Balcárcel coughed, covering his mouth with his napkin, "insists that you join the Youth Front. The elections will be over next month, but the Front will go on collaborating with the Party, and . . ."

"Yes. If you want, I'll go see *Señor* Eusebio in a few days."

"Ay, Jaime, it so good to hear you talking like that!" said Doña Asunción. "You don't know how I've prayed. Listen! Presentación's nephews are giving a party Saturday, and although we are in mourning, it will be all right for you to go if you just eat and don't dance. You're old enough now to meet *señoritas* of your own class and to have a sweetheart . . ."

"Now that you are going to enter Law School, you can begin to work in the office," the uncle coughed again, always with the napkin over his mouth and his eyes avoiding Jaime's. "Some day it will fall upon you to head this house and my businesses. You will learn how pleasant it is to have money earned by your own effort."

"A young man has many obligations," Asunción said, placing her pale hand on Jaime's shoulder. "He must be careful and choose his way well. But don't worry about anything. Though you have lost your father, you still have us and we will take care of you."

"I'm going out for a while," Jaime said, and excused himself. Balcárcel made no comment, and Asunción gave thanks for the new attitudes of the two men.

He slowly went down the stone stairs. No, he would never lie to himself again. He renounced everything and asked for peace. "Now I have no problems, others will do my worrying for me, take care of me, work my life out for me." He came to the door of the stable where he had used to dream, where he had read the books of his adolescence, where he had shut himself up in solitude to gnaw the bones of his visions and thoughts, where he had invented his lies about charity and penance and Christian rebellion. He wanted to say farewell to the dusty beloved old room. But his aunt had locked the door the night before.

He heard Juan Manuel's whistle and went out on the street.

"I took my time last night, Ceballos," Juan Manuel smiled. "When I finished, you were gone."

"Let's walk, Lorenzo."

Would this be the last time they walked the winding narrow alleys together? Jaime felt a profound sense of sadness.

He remembered the ideas they had exchanged when each of them in the middle of adolescence had dared to state without doubt his faith and his decision to act what he believed. Proud owner, each, of a new body, of a new head thinking what had never been thought before. Confident owner, each, of a new will capable of transforming the world. Solitude together, shared loneliness that today would end.

No, he told himself silently as they climbed toward Los Cantaritos, I have loved Juan Manuel, it is not a lie. I never knew my mother, I couldn't really love her. But Juan Manuel he had loved. That was no treason. Juan Manuel was his friend forever, against his aunt and uncle, against the Thursday sewing circle, the priests, the Daughters of Mary.

"I'm leaving Guanajuato, Ceballos . . . I've been offered a better job, with the railroad, in Mexico City. I'm going to join the union. I'll go on studying . . . if I can."

"Juan Manuel."

"Will you look me up, if you are there someday?"

"I wanted so much for us to grow up together."

"We have already grown up together."

"Will we be the same, when we're men?"

"No, Jaime. Our roads are different. Why deceive ourselves?"

"Why do we grow up, Lorenzo? Why? I wish we could always be children. I wish we could always be waiting, holding our secrets inside. Then we would never betray ourselves."

Jaime stopped and faced Juan Manuel.

"I've failed, Lorenzo."

The small brown-skinned youth felt his eyes fill with tears. He was moved by compassion and affection for Jaime, but at the same time he was indignantly angry.

"I'm going to do everything exactly opposite to what I

wanted," Jaime went on. "I'm going to conform, be one in the crowd."

"You won't find anyone that way," Juan Manuel said at last. "Your sorrow isn't serious. Others . . . there are others who really suffer, Ceballos. You don't. Some day you will no longer have the right to set yourself apart from us with the pretext of your own salvation. A great wave of revolution will sweep over your kind and you too. You will find yourself analyzing yourself hopelessly. And the wave will have no respect for you."

"I like you, Lorenzo. You are my friend."

"And I you, Ceballos. Look, I'll give you my address. It's on this paper. Goodbye."

Juan Manuel slipped the paper into Jaime's shirt pocket. The two young friends embraced.

As Juan Manuel walked away, Jaime leaned against the blue wall. His adolescence had ended. For the last time he stared at his small friend's silhouette. Then he turned the corner, repeating softly: "I have come to spread fire over the earth."

He read the address Juan Manuel had given him. *My rooming house: Señora Lola Villegas. Caille de la Espalda de Soto. Number 21, near Avenida Hidalgo.*

He stayed on in the dark alley. What would Juan Manuel have said if he had told him everything? Surely he had understood, there had been no need for words.

"I haven't had the courage. I couldn't be what I wanted to be. I couldn't be a Christian. And I was too weak to stay alone with my failure, I had to find some kind of support, and the only one I have is my aunt and uncle, the life they have prepared for me, the life I inherit. I shall submit myself to established order, in order not to fall into desperation. Forgive me, Ezequiel. Forgive me, Adelina. Forgive me, Juan Manuel."

He realized now that he would be a brilliant law student.

He would pronounce official speeches. He would be the spoiled child of the Party of the Revolution in Guanajuato. He would receive his degree. The city's mighty would consider him a shining example. He would marry a rich girl and found a family. He would live with a good conscience.

A good conscience. This night, in a dark Guanajuato alley, the words crossed his tongue painfully. He was going to be a righteous man. But Christ had not come for the righteous, but for sinners.

For the first time in his life, he denied the idea. No, it wasn't true. He had to become a man now, to give up his childhood illusions. Christ loved the righteous, lived in good consciences, belonged to the just, to the wealthy, to those of fine reputation. Let Satan have the poor and humble, the sinners, the abandoned and miserable, the rebels, everyone who was beyond the pale of gentility.

He walked back to the home of his ancestors. The moon had come out, and Guanajuato's domes and walls and paving stones reflected it not serenely but violently. The great green portal of the Ceballos mansion opened, and Jaime entered.